SOMETHING IN THE WOODSHED

Trussel and Gout: Paranormal Investigations No.2

M.A.Knights

White Harp Publishing

ISBN-13: 9798809280167
ISBN-10: 1477123456

Cover design by M.A.Knights. Images from Shutterstock.
Library of Congress Control Number: 2018675309
Printed in the United States of America

To Burdock, my furry friend who inspired the antics of Custard.

CONTENTS

PART ONE

Mr Gout had not told me everything. That became clear the very first night I arrived to take up my position as his apprentice.

'You sure you want to get off here, miss?' the conductor asked again, sticking his head out of the carriage after me. He shivered in the evening air and pulled the collar of his jacket up around his neck as a powerful gust of wind buffeted the train. 'We don't get many who do.'

He looked warily past me, out into the dark. A solitary, guttering gas lamp lit the central patch of muddy gravel that served as the Abermywl stop. My new home. Beyond it lay darkness, the merest suggestion of undergrowth just visible in the weakest rays of amber light.

'It's okay. I'm meeting someone.' I attempted to keep the hitch out of my voice as a bat fluttered in and out of the lamplight.

The conductor followed it with his eyes. 'It's salt marsh out there, miss. Not something you want to wander into on a night like this.'

I smiled. 'I'm sure Mr Gout will bring a lantern.'

The conductor gave me a long look, then

shrugged. 'A good night to you then, miss.'

He called forward to the driver, then ducked back inside the train, closing the door with a definite clunk. Soon the train was lumbering away with the squeal of metal on metal and a rhythmic chuff-chuff-chuff.

The noise slowly faded under the roar of the wind and the unseen sea. At least the rain, which seemed to have followed me all the way from Fairsop, looked to be finally easing off. The wind, however, showed no signs of letting up. It roared in the darkness, whipping my long hair around my face and making me shiver inside my coat.

I imagined I had known what I was getting myself into. I didn't, of course. But to be fair to my younger self, paranormal investigation is not an easy field to research for the uninitiated. When Theophilius Gout bowled into my world, saving my Granny's life from a horrible monster and introducing me to real magic in the process, was it so surprising that I had jumped at the chance to learn more? I had no idea if I was cut out to be his apprentice. But he offered, and I, fearing my mother would ship me off to a life of domestic servitude if I stayed in the family home much longer, accepted. So there I was. The whole thing had taken several weeks to organise. Then my mother, much to my surprise, had insisted I not leave before Christmas. But eventually the day of departure had come.

It had been a long trip and the train I travelled in had been a warm cocoon against the foulest of nights.

'It's a rum business, this world you're stepping into, Clementine, my dear. Paranormal investigation is not for the faint of heart. You've proven yourself worthy of being my apprentice, but you make sure this is what you really want, hmm?'

Mr Gout's words echoed in my mind and my stomach clenched as I looked around for a sign of someone approaching. But there were no bobbing lights in the distance, no crunch of footsteps on the gravel but my own.

I took a seat on a small wooden bench next to the gas lamp and resolved to wait for my new master's arrival. No doubt he would be along soon. If I truly was fit to be his apprentice, I could not let a stormy January night unsettle me.

I stifled a yawn, opening my bag to retrieve the slice of Battenberg my father had pressed into my hands as I'd left the family bakery that morning. I savoured the sweet taste, trying to ignore the chill creeping into my feet and hands, and thinking of the nightly routine I would be missing back at home for the first time I could remember. The sweeping of the shop. The cleaning down of the bread ovens, ready for the early start in the morning. Chores that would continue on for my parents and brothers, even in my absence. I thought of Granny, no doubt already abed in her small attic room. I hoped my mother had remembered to bring up the warm milk she liked to take before sleep (usually with a good tot of rum she didn't think I saw her add).

I felt bad, lying to my parents. Convincing them about the move to Wales was touch and go as it was, but I doubt they would have agreed to the actual position I was taking. It was best they thought I was simply a housekeeper's apprentice. I could rely on Granny's silence, of course.

Not being able to see much, I used my ears instead, trying to pick out the unfamiliar sound of waves from the wind. Growing up as I had, far from the coast, I was eager for my first glimpse of the mighty Irish sea. But I would have to wait till morning.

As I sat, a creeping unease came over me. I felt as if I was being watched, and kept glancing over my shoulder into the night.

When the cake was gone, I got up and stomped my frozen feet in the darkness a little way off, waiting for my eyes to adjust to the gloom. Slowly, I began to be able to pick out the odd feature. A little dirt path appeared to me, heading off inland, or so I imagined, unless I had completely lost my bearing.

It was then that I heard the faint crunch of gravel, just audible above wind and sea. But I could see nothing. Certainly not the large figure of my new employer. Convinced I'd imagined it, I pulled my coat tighter with a shudder. I took a few tentative steps in the path's direction, nearly jumping out of my skin when the bleat of an animal, unseen but mere feet away, blared out above the storm. Just a sheep, I told myself, waiting for my pumping heart to slow. The roar of the gale flowed back around me.

In the far distance I could see a light I fancied belonged to a house. Deciding I'd had enough of the lonely platform, and my vision having improved to where I felt I was in no immediate danger of walking into the quagmire, I followed the path in that direction.

I edged forward, picking out my way with care and wondering what had prevented Mr Gout from meeting me. Had I got the wrong day? The wrong train? Was he even now impatiently awaiting my arrival on another lonely platform, many miles away, rocking back and forth on his dainty feet, round belly rumbling as he cursed the stupid girl keeping him from his dinner? Had he changed his mind about me entirely? These thoughts and a thousand more flitted through my mind as I trudged along in the darkness, head bent against the wind that stung my face, steadily growing nearer to the lights in the distance.

When I finally reached the house, for a house indeed it was, the front door opened and bright light spilled out across the path in front of me. A man barrelled out of the doorway carrying a storm lantern. He pulled himself up sharply, just avoiding our collision. He cursed in words I didn't understand and, holding the lantern up higher, in a thick Welsh accent called, 'Who goes there?'

'I'm terribly sorry,' I said in a rush. 'I'm afraid I'm a little lost.'

The man's bushy eyebrows rose up his forehead

as he looked at me properly. The wind threatened to wrench the lantern out of his hand and it shook his grey beard back and forth as if trying to detach it from his chin.

'Well, jiw-jiw. Whatever are you doing out alone on a night like this, miss?'

'I've come from the station,' I said. 'Someone was supposed to meet me, but I suppose they've been detained. I don't suppose you know of a Mr Gout, do you?'

Another man appeared silhouetted in the doorway. 'What's going on, Dai? There's no time for chatting, we're needed back at the quay right away!' He peered curiously out at me.

'This girl's come from the station. Says she's looking for Mr Gout,' said the first man; Dai, I supposed.

'The station? On a night like this?' said the second man. 'You want to be careful, miss. There's a devil's wind in the air.'

'That's right enough,' Dai said, nodding. 'Blew a ship onto the rocks not an hour ago, it did.'

'Oh gosh!' I said. 'I hope no one was injured.'

Dai shook his head. 'Not a soul left alive, or so they're saying. But we're needed to search for survivors all the same.'

'And the cargo,' said the second man. 'Spilled her load out like a gutted fish, so she did. Begging your pardon, miss,' he added, apparently remembering he was in the company of a woman.

'Perhaps that is where Mr Gout has gone?' I

suggested.

The man scowled. 'The Englishman? I doubt it.'

Dai tutted. 'Now you leave Mr Gout alone, Gruffydd; he's alright.'

The other man shrugged, but said nothing.

'Mr Gout's place is further up the hill, miss,' Dai continued. 'You just follow the road there and you won't miss it.' He pointed into the night where I could just make out the path I had followed, joining up with a larger track. 'I'd offer to show you the way, only...'

'Oh, it's quite alright, thank you. I wouldn't want to detain you further,' I said, stepping back. Dai seemed torn, but Gruffydd had already closed the door behind him and was heading off down the hill. He shot his companion an impatient look.

'Well, you just go easy now, you hear?' Dai said to me. 'And be sure to give Mr Gout my best. Good man. Fine man. '

'Dai!' Gruffydd called from further back to his friend, where he was already disappearing into the night.

Dai jumped guiltily and moved away. 'Sorry, miss, got to go. Welcome to Abermywl!'

'Thank you!' I called after his retreating back, but he did not turn around.

Soon the two men had vanished, leaving me alone in darkness once more.

Possibly.

The moment they departed, the feeling of being

watched returned. I looked up the dark track I had to travel and shivered. But I had little choice.

I began walking, keeping my eyes firmly on the road in front of me, trying to ignore the thought that something was going to jump out at me from the bushes. There were no lights up ahead and little to guide me, but I trusted that the friendly Dai would not have led me purposefully astray. The road surface was harder and more compacted than the muddy path I had followed thus far. I listened to the sound of my own footsteps, the wind whistling through unseen trees, and the distant roar of the sea as I trudged wearily up the hill.

But there was something else. Something almost not there at all. Just on the edge of hearing.

The tiny tap-tap-tap of little feet on the road behind me.

The hairs on the back of my neck began to prickle. My fear overcame my resolve and I flashed a nervous look over my shoulder. Nothing. Perhaps another sheep, I thought. An escapee down on the road somewhere.

I pressed on, quickening my pace and humming slightly under my breath to calm my nerves.

But in between each breath, I could still hear it.

Tap-tap-tap. Tap-tap-tap.

I sped up again, practically trotting through the darkness now. I reached a gap in the hedge to my right and the icy wind whipped through it across my face, making me turn my head away in shock.

Then I saw it.

A weak, flickering light off to my left. I hurried closer and with relief saw a little stone cottage set back some way from the road. It nestled into the hillside like one of the sheep sheltering out in the darkness. I had almost walked right past it in my haste. At the roadside was a low wall, and beyond that I could just make out the impression of raised vegetable beds, and a garden path running between them. The house itself could almost have seemed empty. There was just one pale light, the light that had caught my eye, from a lantern or similar placed somewhere in the front room. The only other sign of life was a thin stream of smoke issuing from the chimney, bent at a sharp angle by the wind.

Supposing that this must be the place – and frankly thinking that any house was better than one more minute out in the storm – I took a last look over my shoulder, then hurried down the path. I stopped before the wooden front door and rapped it sharply with a trembling hand.

The door flew open almost the second I withdrew my knuckles and the bulbous form of Mr Gout filled its frame. He was dressed in tweed, as was his custom, but his jacket had been removed and his shirtsleeves trailed unbuttoned from his forearms. There was a large brown stain down his usually immaculate waistcoat.

'Um, good evening, sir,' I said, slightly taken aback.

The tall man looked down at me, his eyes large and uncomprehending. Then his mouth dropped open and he slapped a chubby hand to his forehead.

'Miss Trussel! My goodness, you poor girl, I had quite forgotten the time. Come in, come in!' He practically dragged me through the door, slamming it behind me, gabbling away as he did so. 'What you must think of me, my dear girl. And on a night like this! Why, I am quite ashamed. But here you are! Splendid, splendid. Welcome to Oystercatcher Cottage. Good trip, was it? I do like a train journey. Quite the superior way to travel, I always say. Yes, yes indeed. Quite superior!'

His manner was so excitable, his eyes so wild, that it was a moment or two before I dragged my own away from his face to look at the room I had been ushered into.

I had thought much in the preceding days and weeks of the home of my new master. It was hard to picture the type of room that might hold the remarkable personality of a man such as he. But whatever I had imagined, it was not this.

We had stepped into a parlour, much of which was filled by the frame of Mr Gout himself. One corner was taken up by a simple kitchen range, and yet more space was sacrificed by the inclusion of a large wooden table. All disappointingly plain, had it not been for the scene of destruction that lay before us. On the table had been spilt a large pot of soup, which had spread across the surface and was now dripping onto the stone floor, quite unheeded. The kitchen cupboards were all open, one door hanging from a single hinge, and their contents spilling out to mix with the soup. On the opposite wall was a stone fireplace. Neat little trinkets were placed at precise intervals across its simple mantle, but the fire itself had been left to smoke excessively and some of the half-burned wood had spilled out onto the little rug that lay before it. A solitary oil lamp lit the scene.

Perhaps noticing my startled expression, Mr Gout looked up and surveyed the chaos as if seeing it for the first time. 'Ah, yes. Pity. I'm afraid you join us at a delicate moment, Clementine, my dear.'

I was about to enquire further, but at that moment there came a crash and a strangled cry from out of sight in the adjoining room. Something blue shot into the little parlour, followed by an old black woman brandishing what appeared to be some sort of butterfly net. She had dishevelled, frizzy, grey hair and two sea-grey eyes that gleamed in fury out of a face the colour of burnt caramel. With another cry through gritted teeth, she launched herself towards the table and brought her net down onto the soup-covered surface with a thud and a splat. There was another flash of blue as something leapt from the table surface and landed on the rug by the fire.

Now it was time for my mouth to drop open.

Sat on the little rug, twitching its nose and somehow conveying a sense of intense satisfaction, was a large rabbit. It glowed with a greeny-blue light and I could see the soot-stained rug clearly through its translucent body.

'What…' I trailed off, unsure what to say.

Mr Gout beamed. 'This is Custard, my pet rabbit.'

'But...but it's...'

'Dead?' snapped the old woman, straightening up and attempting to smooth her wild hair with little success. 'Oh, quite.'

'You mean...it's a—'

'Ghost? Yes. Poltergeist, to be precise. And a bloody menace!' Her accent was just as strongly Welsh as Dai's had been. The woman turned to Mr Gout with a disapproving expression. 'Who's this?'

Mr Gout's smile melted into a distinctly guilty expression. 'Ah...yes. This is Miss Trussel. Clementine, my dear, may I introduce the estimable Mrs Winchester, my housekeeper and, more importantly, of course, my dear, dear friend.'

Mrs Winchester cocked a thin eyebrow.

'I'm very pleased to meet you.' Dragging my eyes away from the ghostly Custard, who was now unconcernedly washing its ears in front of the smoking fire, I gave a little curtsy. 'I look forward to working with you.'

At that an ugly scowl fell across Mrs Winchester's face. 'What's that?' she snapped, her words like the white-hot point of a welding iron.

Mr Gout shifted awkwardly and tapped his fingertips together in front of his chest. 'Ah, well...that is...I thought...well, the thing is...' he floundered, his chin wobbling as his mouth opened and shut uncertainly.

'You're replacing me, ain't you?' Mrs Winchester said before he could complete a sentence. 'Tired of looking at me, are you? Fed up of these old bones? Thought you'd get a younger model in, did you? Some fancy miss to bow and curtsy while she serves your supper? Well, I'll tell you now, you fat old lizard, I'll not be going quietly! You wait till you see what ole Mrs A Winchester is capable of!'

Mr Gout looked stricken. 'No, no, no! My dear woman, you have quite got the wrong end of the stick. Replace you? Never! Never, my dear Mrs Winchester, pray perish the thought. Why, you are as dear to me as...as...'

'As what?' Mrs Winchester's eyes narrowed, her voice quiet now, and all the more terrible for it.

Mr Gout's eyes roved around desperately as he searched for inspiration. 'As the hair upon my very head!' he finished, rather lamely.

Mrs Winchester sniffed. 'You should have said your stomach, you great glutton. That might have meant something.' But the white heat of her anger seemed to have cooled slightly and now glowed a cherry red. 'Well, if I'm not to be replaced, then who is she?'

'A most competent young woman who helped me with that case in Fairsop,' said Mr Gout, sounding relieved. 'I've taken her as my apprentice, and...well, if she finds the time to help you with a chore or two while she's here, then I'm sure you won't object.'

Mrs Winchester's expression said she wasn't so sure, but when she turned her eyes back to me, there was a measure or two less hostility. 'Apprentice, is it?' She looked me up and down appraisingly, taking in my bedraggled brown hair, skinny frame, dress, and pinny. 'We'll see.'

There was an uncomfortable silence as the formidable woman's eyes lingered on me. Then, with no warning at all, her gaze shifted back to the deceased rabbit in front of the fire. 'Now, what are you going to do about that infernal animal?'

'Um…do?' said Mr Gout, paling again.

'Just look at the state of this place!' the housekeeper said. 'The detestable thing's gone rogue!'

A hurt expression appeared on Mr Gout's round face. 'He doesn't mean anything by it, do you, Custard?'

The rabbit looked up, wrinkled its nose, and then – and I swear this is true – stuck its tiny tongue out.

'This really is intolerable, Theophilius,' Mrs Winchester snapped. 'The infernal thing keeps jumping out at me. I think it's trying to give me a heart attack.'

'He's just excited.' Mr Gout smiled fondly at the rabbit, which had now hopped under the table and was sniffing enthusiastically at the spilt soup. 'He was seventeen, you know, quite an age for a rabbit. I think he's just happy to be free of the arthritis!' he said to me with another smile.

'Hmmm,' Mrs Winchester said. 'Don't know when it's worn out its welcome, if you ask me.' Then she pointed to an old green teapot that sat at the end of the table, remarkably unscathed. 'Tea,' she announced.

Dinner that first night was a late and somewhat strained affair. Mrs Winchester insisted on mopping up some of the mess Custard had caused first and would not allow either Mr Gout or myself to help. I sat awkwardly in a wooden chair by the fire (now cleaned and stoked) sipping lukewarm tea from a fragile china cup I'd had to serve myself. Mrs Winchester, it seemed, had somehow forgotten me.

'You'll soon feel at home,' Mr Gout said, sitting opposite in a high-backed armchair and smiling encouragingly.

I watched the ghostly Custard, now sleeping at his feet, and wondered if that was true.

Dinner, when it arrived, was the bread that had been meant to go with the soup. Mrs Winchester also found a little cheese and a dusty fruitcake she proudly announced as bara brith.

Mr Gout looked at the fare forlornly. 'Is this all?'

Mrs Winchester glowered at him; I was starting to suspect this was her go-to expression. 'It's my shopping day tomorrow. Good job too, as now I've another mouth to feed!'

Mr Gout looked about to protest, but then thought better of it. Instead he shot a bright smile in my direction. 'Well, perhaps you could whip us up one of your famous Victoria sponges this evening, Miss Trussel?'

Mrs Winchester had returned to her supper, but at this her head snapped back around in his direction. 'What's this now?'

'Clementine's a master baker,' Mr Gout explained. 'Her parents' bakery sells the most–'

Mrs Winchester slapped the tabletop with a clatter. 'You *are* trying to replace me! I do the cooking around here. Me! I've always done the cooking. That's part of the arrangement. Now suddenly it's not good enough for you?'

Mr Gout started, his mouth halfway around a large hunk of bread. He swallowed hastily and, sounding wretched, said, 'I just thought it might be nice to have a baker in the house. That side of things has never...well...you're more of a stew and dumplings woman...'

'A. Stew. And. Dumplings. Woman.' Mrs Winchester quivered with barely repressed rage.

Mr Gout sprung to his feet and bounced across the room with a speed belied by his generous girth. In a moment he stood by a door at the back of the room, which, judging by the small circular window within it, led outside to the back of the property. 'I think perhaps I'll take my supper to my study,' he said in a rush, groping at the door handle. 'Do make yourself at home, Clementine, dear.'

The door opened, and he ducked through it, just in time for the green teapot to come sailing over his head and smash on something unseen. The door slammed closed, and I was left in a ringing silence while Mrs Winchester glared daggers at the closed door.

'Well then,' she said eventually. 'I suppose I'd better make up the spare bed. You'll come shopping with me in the morning, girl. I'll need help to carry the extra food. Oh, and we'll be needing a new teapot.'

The storm blew itself out at around midnight. The spare bed, as it turned out, was a mattress laid out in front of the fireplace. I lay awake next to the dying embers, looking at the shadowy kitchen cupboards, still in disarray, and thinking of my cosy room back at home. Mr Gout had not reappeared, and the remainder of the evening had been spent in silence. Mrs Winchester and I had one brief interlude where the housekeeper caught me looking at her and snapped, 'Half Welsh, half Gambian. Something to say about it?'

I shook my head, mutely terrified.

After that, I dared not look at her again. Mrs Winchester knitted in a passive aggressive manner, something I had not heretofore realised was possible, the click-clack of the needles becoming so unbearable that I had welcomed bedtime with relief.

I'd been sent out back to collect more firewood, using the door through which Mr Gout had disappeared. Behind the house a rough little track ran up the steep hill and disappeared. I could see no sign of a study, but I did discover a small rickety woodshed with a rusty corrugated iron roof. I don't know if it was the quality of the now still night, or the deep inky blackness that filled the wonky doorway, but I approached the little building with trepidation. The feeling of being watched, which

I had quite forgotten about in all the excitement, returned. I fancied I could hear something snuffling about inside. My bravery deserting me, I grabbed the few bits of wood lying on the ground outside and dashed back to the house.

PART TWO

Early the next morning, we awoke to a shock. Mrs Winchester entered the parlour and gave a shriek of outrage.

'What you done?'

Still bleary-eyed, I lifted my head from the mattress. 'I'm sorry?'

'The kitchen, girl!'

I looked over. Then rubbed the sleep out of my eyes and looked again. During the night the cupboards had been fixed. Not only fixed, but scrubbed furiously clean so that they positively gleamed in the pale morning light. Mrs Winchester bustled over and threw open the doors. Neatly sorted boxes, packets and jars were revealed. Porridge oats nestled snugly against strawberry jam, sugar against the tea – a far cry from the chaos of the previous evening.

'You've no right!' she slammed the doors closed again. 'No right at all!'

'But...but I didn't!' I said. 'Mr Gout...perhaps he...?'

The housekeeper shot me a filthy look. 'You think I was born yesterday, girl? Theophilius doesn't know a duster from a handkerchief. I know what you're about, and I won't be standing for it!'

We left the house soon after, the mystery unexplained, although it was clear that my protestations of innocence were falling on deaf ears.

Of Mr Gout, there was still no sign.

Despite her assertion that we were going shopping, Mrs Winchester led me along a scrubby, exposed coastal path. Though the worst of the storm had blown itself out, the wind and rain still whipped at my hair, and every few paces I had to pull it out of my eyes to avoid stumbling. Mrs Winchester's own tight grey curls merely shook this way and that, never once interfering with her vision, and she stalked along the cliff edge at a pace that had me feeling queasy.

When I wasn't blinded by my hair or watching my own feet, I snuck awestruck glances out to sea. I'd thought myself somewhat prepared for my first view of the ocean. I'd seen pictures. Mrs Hanover, back in Fairsop, had a watercolour of a beach above her mantlepiece. Sun, sand, and bright little flowers amongst the dunes. But this was moody blue-green water that spread out in front of us like an undiscovered country. The sand was the grey colour of old dough. Wavy peaks formed like soft meringue, giving me a pang of homesickness for my parents' bakery. Black rocks, like enormous pieces of coal, stuck up out of the water all along the coastline, rimmed with the frothing white of the waves. The cliffs themselves were a series of sharp, jagged lines in crisscrossing patterns, so close to being geometric they almost looked carved by human hands. I could smell salt on the wind and heard the harsh cry of seagulls that swooped over our heads. Above everything was the rhythmic crashing of the waves.

We came to a horseshoe-shaped cove, deserted, except for an improbable tree trunk, left stranded halfway up the beach, and a handful of small brown birds that flew low over the tideline, hopping and pecking amongst the purple and green seaweed. I followed Mrs Winchester, who offered no explanation as to our destination, down a zig-zag path that was little more than a rock scramble. We stepped out onto the beach and I almost immediately stumbled. I'd never walked on sand before. It was coarse, a mixture of minuscule pebbles, green, blue, white, purple and grey. I thought of Mrs Hanover's watercolour and its bright golden sands. I wondered if the artist had ever actually been to a beach before.

Mrs Winchester strode purposefully across the sand without a backwards look. She dropped her little string bag by the abandoned tree trunk, which I could now see was worn smooth and pale by the water. I wondered how many tides it had been subjected to. Where had it come from? How did it end up here?

Then, to my utter astonishment, Mrs Winchester began to remove her clothes.

'W...what are you doing?' I gasped, looking

around in case anyone was watching from the cliffs above.

'What's it look like I'm doing, my girl?'

Mrs Winchester's voice was muffled slightly as she pulled her blouse over her head, not bothering to undo most of the buttons. Her thick shawl already lay on the sand and she swiftly kicked off her shoes to join it, stepping out of her dress in a practised motion. Her stockings quickly followed until she stood before me, hands on her hips, in nothing but her white camisole and bloomers. They contrasted starkly against her dark skin. She looked at my astonishment and the corner of her mouth quirked up into the nearest thing to a smile I had so far seen on her wrinkled face. Then she turned her back on me, removed the final pieces of her clothing and marched, quite naked, towards the sea.

She waded into the dark water, calling over her shoulder, 'Cold water's good for the body and mind, girl. You should join me. It'd do your constitution the world of good, I don't doubt.'

But she didn't wait to see if I'd take up her offer, striding through the waves until they lapped around her shoulders, then pushing forward and swimming off without a backwards glance.

I looked around anxiously, but there was still no one else in sight. Was she safe out there? It didn't seem safe. At her age, too! I followed her to the waterline but stopped short of where the tendrils of the latest wave were soaking into the sand. Nothing about the water looked inviting to me and I shuddered with the chill just watching the housekeeper, who was now doing a confident backstroke back and forth between the rock walls of the cove.

She was trying to shock me, I decided. Or shame me somehow. Well, I wasn't going to let her get the better of me!

I kicked off my shoes and walked hesitantly forward into the oncoming wave. The water sloshed over my feet and I actually cried out in surprise and pain at the cold. Was the old goat crazy? My pride forgotten, I hopped and skipped back out of the water, but my face burned when I heard a chuckling above the sound of the waves. I scooped up my shoes and stomped back to the old tree trunk in bad grace. I sat and attempted to brush the coarse sand from my wet feet so I could put my shoes back on, but it turned out to be an impossible task.

It was then that I looked up and saw the silhouette of a man standing on the cliffs, looking down into the bay. He waved, then shouted down to me.

'I wouldn't feel bad. We're not all as hardy as Mrs Winchester there. You wouldn't catch me in the sea this time of year!' And then he laughed; a great booming sound that echoed around the cove, only seeming to stop when it was drowned out by the slap of a large wave against a fold in the rocks. I squinted up at the man, holding my hand above my eyes to protect them from the rain and so see this newcomer better. He was a mature man, perhaps in his fifties, with a salt and pepper beard and a peaked cap on his head. He wore a blue jacket and a pair of bright yellow waders. He looked...well, one doesn't like to reinforce stereotypes, but if Mrs Hanover's watercolour had included a jolly fisherman, they would have looked just like this man.

I stood, sneaking a glance at the distant Mrs Winchester, still ploughing through the waves. Still naked. When I didn't reply, the man called down again.

'It's Dai. I believe we met last night, Miss, er...?'

I realised it was indeed the man I had met on the dark track the night before. 'Miss Trussel!' I called up to him, not wanting to appear rude. 'Nice to meet you again, sir.'

The man waved again, then began his descent into the cove. When he reached me, he nodded and touched his cap. 'You staying with Mr Gout then, Miss Trussel?'

'I'm his new assistant house ke...his new apprentice,' I said, correcting myself with a surge of defiant pride. I wasn't entirely sure if Mr Gout's profession was common knowledge, but he hadn't asked me to keep it a secret. Any doubts I had on that score, however, melted away when I saw Dai's eyes widen, and he said, 'Are you indeed? Well, well. Interesting work, I don't doubt. Fine man, Mr Gout, as I said last night. He helped me out with a little Siren trouble a few years ago.'

'That's nice,' I said politely.

Dai grimaced. 'It certainly wasn't at the time!'

At that moment Mrs Winchester emerged, dripping, from the water and marched up the beach, quite unabashed.

'What you doing here, Dai?' She made no effort to cover herself.

'I've brought your usual fish order, Angharad,' the man said, producing a brown parcel from inside his coat. 'It's no day for anyone to be down on the quayside today. Quite the hullabaloo, so there is.'

'Did you find any survivors last night?' I asked.

Dai grimaced and rubbed his neck with one hand. 'We did, as it happens, miss. One.'

'Well, you don't look very happy about it,' Mrs Winchester observed, beginning to dress herself.

'Truth be told, if it were up to me, I'd have half a mind to throw the wretch back in the sea.'

'Why, Mr Thomas, whatever do you mean by that?' Mrs Winchester paused at her buttons and looked affronted. 'I know you to be a man with more compassion. I'd expect a comment like that from Gruffydd Pew, but not from you!'

'I know, I know,' the fisherman said, looking wretched. 'But to be perfectly honest, I don't know if it wouldn't be doing the poor man a favour. Raving, he is, quite raving. Can't get no sense out of him.'

'Well, you know more than most what the sea can do to a man,' said Mrs Winchester.

'That's true,' Dai admitted. But then he shuddered. 'But you didn't see him when we found him. Three quarters dead, he was. Cut up by rocks. Leg broken. They've still got him in one of the sheds down by the quay, trying to warm some life back into him. But it was his eyes that got me. Blank, they were. Something broke that man and I reckon it happened before the water got to him.'

Mrs Winchester tutted. 'Well, now you sound like some superstitious old fishwife.'

'It ain't superstition if you know it's real,' Dai said with a sniff. 'There's more in them waters than fish.'

'Do you know what caused the ship to sink?' I asked.

Dai shrugged. 'It blew it off course and onto the rocks. Ain't no mystery there. Storms can come on sudden in these parts, miss.'

'What does the survivor say happened?'

Dai grimaced. 'He don't. Not coherently, anyway. Just keeps muttering the same word. Klabautermann...over and over. Sounds foreign. No idea what it means.'

'Well, as fascinating as this all is, it's not getting the shopping done,' said Mrs Winchester, now fully clothed once more.

Dai handed her the parcel, rubbing his neck again with his free hand. 'I figured you might still have Miss Trussel here with you, so I slipped in an extra couple of herrings. Nice fat ones.'

Mrs Winchester nodded her thanks. 'I'm much obliged to you, Dai. You alright?'

Dai gave another shrug. 'Oh, it's nothing, just a stiff neck. It's been a long night. Well, I'd best get back. They're still fishing all kinds of stuff out of the salt marsh, and Old Farmer Jones will be tamping if one of his precious ewes chokes on something other than its own tongue. No rest for the wicked, dear ladies, no rest for the wicked!'

After parting with Mr Thomas, Mrs Winchester led me into the village and we did the shopping as she'd promised. I followed her from grocer to baker to butcher, down the gently sloping road that passed for the hub of Abermywl. The road didn't so much end as simply run right into the gently lapping waters of the estuary onto which the village clung. Little row boats bobbed about in the shallows and further up the river I could make out a large four-storied stone building that must have been the quay warehouse. There did seem to be a buzz of activity around the place, but in the village we met as many seagulls as we did people. Those we came into contact with were wrapped up well against the weather; the women in thick shawls, most of the men sporting stiff waxed waders and coats. They greeted my guide with the same words, in tones that ranged from friendly to tight politeness. Mrs Winchester would grunt back, or wave, never once bothering to stop and introduce me. The words meant nothing to me, Welsh still being a strange, guttural language to my foreign ears. But after the fourth repetition I began to recognise the greeting and resolved to try it out for myself.

Towards the water sat a squat, single-roomed public house by the name of The Ship and Cockle. It looked as if it had been built a long time ago from whatever bits of stone happened to be lying around. As we entered, I muttered a hesitant 'Bore da,' to the windswept-looking man behind the bar, trying not to choke on the strong fug of tobacco smoke that filled the stale air. He looked at me strangely for a moment, then his tanned face split into a welcoming smile.

'Bore da, to you too, young miss. Always a pleasure to hear the Welsh tongue from the lips of a traveller. Malwyn Pottersburgh, at your service.'

Mrs Winchester shot me an unreadable look, then turned back to the barman. 'The usual please, Mal.'

'And for you, miss...?' said the barman.

'Trussel,' I said, then hesitated. In truth, I was unused to being in a public house without the company of my parents, particularly my father. I looked around the small room and saw several male drinkers, all of whom were regarding us with interest. There didn't seem to be any outright hostility, however. 'I'll have the same, please; thank you.'

Mrs Winchester made a little noise in her throat that might have been a laugh or simply a cough. I decided on the former, when, five minutes later, we were seated at a small, round wooden table in one corner and Mal deposited two pints of dark, frothy ale in front of us.

'Iechyd da!' Mrs Winchester saluted me with her glass, an amused expression on her face. I looked at my drink and tried not to show my dismay. I had tried ale before, of course, but had little taste for it, and had certainly never consumed an entire pint. My companion was already quaffing hers with every sign of enjoyment, so I lifted my glass and took an experimental sip. The bitter notes hit my tongue, and I nearly choked as a loud, angry voice said, 'That ain't right!' I hastily wiped the foam from my lips and turned to see that the door had opened and Gruffydd Pew was staring right at us, looking furious.

Behind the bar, Mal had adopted an expression of long-suffering annoyance. 'Come in, if you're coming, Gruff.'

Mr Pew glowered at him. 'You're just going to allow this, are you? Two women, drinking alone. And worse than that, two foreigners!'

The bartender spat out a curse I didn't understand, drawing a hand across his face. I got the distinct impression this was an argument had many times before. 'As you know very well, this pub welcomes any friendly face. Now shut yours before I decide that doesn't include you!'

Mr Pew shook his head in disbelief, but let the door swing shut, depositing himself at a table. There was silence in the little room as Mal drew a pint and then deposited it in front of the newcomer. I looked to Mrs Winchester, but she was gazing out of the window as if she hadn't heard a thing. I stared at the popping foam on the top of my glass, feeling distinctly uncomfortable, until another patron broached a question that made me look up again.

'How goes it at the quay, Gruff?'

Mr Pew made a face. 'Ain't nothing to do with me no more, is it? You know how it is.'

There were various nods around the room, indicating that the rest of the pub's patrons did indeed know how it was, even if I didn't.

Pew took a long pull at his beer and then belched loudly. 'Bunch of outsiders, swarming around, giving out orders. Well, I ain't taking orders from no Saes!'

'Gruff!' Mal snapped, with a nervous look in our direction.

Mr Pew fell silent and gradually a gentle murmur of conversation filled the room once more.

Mal sidled over to our table, looking apologetic. 'You take no notice of Gruff, miss,' he said to me, fussing at the tabletop with a damp rag. 'He don't speak for the rest of us. Well, not all of us, anyway.'

'What does Saes mean?' I asked, which caused the bartender to stop pretending to clean the table and simply run the filthy rag through his hands agitatedly, refusing to meet my eye.

'Oh, you don't want to worry about that, miss.'

'He's talking about the English,' Mrs Winchester said, still staring out the window.

'Oh.' Embarrassed, I looked down at my beer once more.

'Like I said, miss, you pay him no mind. Head stuck in the past, that one,' Mal said with an encouraging smile. One of his other patrons called across to him in Welsh, brandishing an empty glass. Mal made a quick shooing motion over his shoulder, shouting, 'Alright, alright, bach! I'll be there now, in a minute,' before turning back to me, an earnest expression on his face. 'Besides, any friend of Mr Gout's is welcome in my pub. I count myself lucky to be one myself.'

'Th...thank you,' I said, still feeling uncomfortable.

Mal beamed and turned to Mrs Winchester. 'We go back a long way, Theophilius and I. Ain't that right, Angharad?'

But Mrs Winchester ignored him, her gaze still fixed on something outside the window. The publican followed her line of sight and his smile faltered. He said something that sounded to my inexperienced ears like 'Uh-ka-vee!' and whistled low under his breath. 'Who's that poor bugger?'

I looked out the window. The glass was thick and warped, but you could just see the point where the road met the water from our position. Standing in the shallows was a small cluster of figures who had evidently just climbed out of a little rowing boat. It was now gently knocking against the slope of dry land with the ebb of the water.

I could tell immediately which of them Mal had been referring to, for in the centre of the group slouched the most painfully thin man I had ever seen. He was wrapped in a stiff-looking woollen blanket, thin grey tendrils of hair framing his gaunt face.

'I think that is the man they pulled from the sea last night,' I said.

The other men, as they busied themselves with the boat and a number of little parcels, seemed to be unconsciously keeping their distance from him, as though he were enclosed by some invisible bubble. But as I watched, one of them – Dai the fisherman, as it turned out – did approach him. The survivor made to take a step forward, but Dai hurried to place a restraining hand on his chest. The emaciated figure reacted slowly to the touch, only seeming to notice Dai's presence several seconds after the hand had been placed. He turned to look at him and I got my first clear view of the man's sunken eyes. Dai had been right. They looked empty, as if he were barely aware of his surroundings.

Dai called to one of the other men and between them they supported the injured man, helping him walk. Their course would take them right past the pub window, and the three of us watched as they grew closer.

Mal whistled. 'I've seen a few wash up in my years in Abermywl, but ain't a one of them looked in such a bad way as that fellow. He looks haunted.'

Mr Pew gave a short bark of a laugh behind us. 'Haunted is right. His mind's gone, that one.'

'He's so thin,' I said.

Mal nodded. 'Yes. Must have been a rough voyage, even before the ship went down.'

The figures outside were passing the window now. I couldn't take my eyes off the shipwrecked man. He lurched along between his supporters, one leg trailing uselessly behind him.

Then, just as he was at the closest point to the pub that their path would take, he stiffened. It was like watching a cat who had suddenly smelt a mouse. His head whipped round to face us and, for a second, his eyes looked directly into mine. For that brief moment the victim, the poor, forlorn survivor of a terrible accident, was gone, and in his place was a man whose eyes – empty mere moments before – now flared at me with a savage hunger. I started backwards, but before I knew it, the man had turned away and the procession continued past.

Mal patted me gently on the shoulder. 'Not to worry. He gave me a start en'll.'

We watched in silence as the group shuffled off. Then I jumped again as Mrs Winchester brought her empty glass down on the table with a bang. 'Time to go,' she announced.

PART THREE

After completing the rest of our shopping, we returned to Oystercatcher Cottage to find Custard had got into the pantry and eaten all the carrots. It wasn't something I had expected a ghost to be able to do. After all...where did it all go? A little trail of neglected orange crumbs led up to the ghostly culprit, where he lay sleeping in front of the smouldering fire. Mr Gout was sitting at the table, which was covered in books and papers. He didn't so much as look up when we entered.

'Oh, for the love of...Mr Gout! Could you not have stopped him?' Mrs Winchester slammed down the parcel of fish onto an inch of empty tabletop.

'Ah, Mrs Winchester, Miss Trussel, how nice to see you!' he said, still not looking up. 'Stop who, my dear lady?'

'That flea-bitten thing you call a rabbit!'

'Flea-bitten?' Mr Gout said, finally tearing his eyes away from what he was reading. 'What a simply fascinating idea. Are you postulating that some of the little *Spilopsyllus cuniculi* might have made the transition over to the spirit realm with him?'

'What I'm postulating, Theophilius, is that if you don't find a way to control that damn bunny, I'll personally be performing an exorcism on it!'

'You kept this?' I said, ignoring their bickering. I had just spotted something familiar amidst the literary detritus on the table and picked it up. It was a large green feather, one I was certain I had last seen poking out of a derby hat worn by a pig.

Mr Gout focused his attention on me. 'Ah yes, our porcine friend's feather. I've been doing some research since our first adventure. You'll recall, of course, the sigil we found?'

I looked at the small image painted on the feather in purple ink. A single lily. I nodded. 'Of course. You said you had seen it before. Have you remembered where?'

Mr Gout sighed. 'Alas not. I just know I've seen the image somewhere before, but the memory eludes me.'

There was something off about the way he said it. I was just trying to decide what it was when my thoughts were interrupted.

'Where's the fish?' Mrs Winchester had been bustling around the kitchen, but now stood in front of the empty patch of table where the fish had been placed, scowling at me with her hands on her hips.

'I...I haven't touched it,' I said, surprised.

'Well, it didn't swim off by itself!' she snapped.

Mr Gout gave a small smile. 'Perhaps you already put it away?'

'Nonsense! You might be scatter-brained, you old

sot, but there ain't nothing wrong with my memory. If the girl didn't move it, then it was that sodding rabbit!'

'Custard is a herbivore, Mrs Winchester, and therefore unlikely to have much interest in fish,' Mr Gout said coolly, then smiled. 'Fear not, my dear, I'm sure they'll turn up.'

But they didn't, and Mrs Winchester spent the rest of the day thundering about the place, muttering to herself, opening and shutting cupboards, picking things up and looking under them, attempting to interrogate the uncooperative Custard, and shooting suspicious looks in my direction.

I did my best to ignore her, sitting at the table with Mr Gout, sipping tea and trying to make sense of the many books in front of me. They had titles like *Professor Periwinkle's Precise Compendium of Secret Signs and Sigils*, and *Runes for the Novice Witch: How to hex your friends and influence people*, quite unlike anything I had come across before. But then what else had I expected? This was the house of a paranormal investigator. It made sense that his library might be...well, a little unusual.

Truth be told, I was feeling a bit useless. Mr Gout had given no indication what he wanted me to do, and I dared not attempt to help Mrs Winchester. I was about to pluck up the courage to ask Mr Gout for a little direction when there came an outraged cry from somewhere out in the front garden, then a furious Mrs Winchester exploded through the front door and back into the parlour. The noise was loud enough to disturb even the studious Mr Gout. He looked up with a perplexed expression at the trembling housekeeper, who was covered in what appeared to be soot.

'My dear lady, whatever is the matter?' he asked.

'The chimney!' Mrs Winchester said, shaking. 'She's put them in the bloody chimney to smoke!'

'Who, and what?' Mr Gout asked, the picture of calm.

'The fish, you stupid man! Your supposed apprentice has put them in the chimney to smoke, without my permission!'

'I did no such thing!' I protested. These constant accusations were beginning to get on my nerves.

'Did you not want them smoked?' A slight wrinkle of incomprehension sat between Mr Gout's eyes.

Mrs Winchester hesitated for a moment. 'That… that's not the point!'

'So you did want them smoked?'

'Well, yes, but she had no right to do it! Not her job. Not her place. Sneaking around behind my back. Undermining me. I won't stand for it, I tell you!'

'I do not sneak!' I said, getting to my feet and facing the fuming old woman. 'And I already told you, I never touched your stupid fish.'

'There you go then,' Mr Gout said, appealing for calm. 'I'm sure Miss Trussel wouldn't lie.'

'I don't trust her,' Mrs Winchester said. 'And a

rabbit couldn't have done it, dead or otherwise.'

'Well, I'm sure there is a perfectly reasonable explanation–' Mr Gout tried, but the old woman cut him off.

'Of course there is! This little...little...' she floundered, apparently searching for the right word.

My eyes narrowed. 'Little what?'

Mrs Winchester fixed me with her grey-green eyes and pursed her thin lips. 'Little wagtail!' she snapped.

There was a loud bang and a scraping sound as Mr Gout's chair flung backward and he shot to his feet, catching the table with his belly and buffeting it across the flagstone floor, sending books scattering. 'MRS WINCHESTER, YOU FORGET YOURSELF!' he boomed, face furious. The change in his demeanour was so sudden and unexpected that it made me jump. Mrs Winchester paled under the baleful glare of her usually jovial employer.

'Miss Trussel, would you be so kind as to fetch some more wood for the fire? The good Mrs Winchester and myself require a moment alone for a little chat,' he said in more familiar tones, not removing his stony gaze from the housekeeper.

I left without daring to utter a word, closing the back door quietly behind me and leaning against it, stunned. I found myself more shocked by Mr Gout's outburst than by Mrs Winchester's insults. It seemed there was a limit to his good humour. It was nice of him to stand up for me, but I felt a little wretched at having been the cause of his and

Mrs Winchester's falling out. Then again, I wasn't the cause, I reminded myself. I really hadn't touched the fish. Nor cleaned the cupboards that morning. I was beginning to suspect there was something fishy going on, no pun intended.

That suspicion intensified when a familiar feeling of being observed fell over me and I looked up to see a neatly stacked pile of freshly chopped firewood outside the woodshed. I felt sure it had not been there earlier, and I doubted very much that Mr Gout was given to hefting axes.

My blood still running a little hot, I stamped over to the dilapidated shed and demanded, 'Who's there! This isn't funny, you know!' in a shaky voice. I got no response, but I fancied I could just hear the movement of little feet in the darkened building. I also caught a scent, the very particular, fishy, swampy scent of the salt marsh I had noticed for the first time just the night before, as I stood on the Abermywl station platform. The kernel of an idea began to form.

When I returned to the house with my arms full of firewood, a distinctly awkward atmosphere prevailed. Mrs Winchester busied herself at the kitchen sink and did not look around when I entered. Mr Gout beamed at me, but said nothing. I set to with the fire, then resumed my seat at the table in silence. Eventually, I plucked up the courage to speak.

'Mr Gout, I wondered if you knew what the word

Klabautermann meant.'

Mr Gout put down the book he was reading and scratched his fleshy chin. 'Well now, let me think. Klabautermann...Klabautermann.... Ah, yes! If I recall, my dear, a Klabautermann is a specific type of Kobold said to be found on ships.'

'Oh,' I said. 'And what is a Kobold?'

'Ah, well now, a Kobold, or Cofgod in the old English if you prefer...?' He paused and looked at me inquiringly.

Feeling something was expected of me, I shrugged. 'Kobold is fine.'

Mr Gout nodded and continued his explanation. 'A Kobold is thought to be a sort of spirit or sprite. Some even call them gods, although that seems a little hyperbolic for my taste, most commonly found in the homes of humans. Sometimes reported as good luck charms. A foolish miscalculation, in my opinion.'

I swallowed, an uneasy feeling creeping over me. 'They're dangerous?'

'That depends. The legends speak of some being very helpful to their human hosts, warning of danger, bringing financial fortune, that sort of thing. But if you read further, you'll see there's far more to it than that. They're very particular creatures. Very proud. The texts say they expect certain privileges for the help they provide, and if you make even a minor mistake, their anger can be fierce. They're not above murder in some instances! All in all, best left alone in my opinion. You certainly

SOMETHING IN THE WOODSHED

shouldn't ever cross one or encourage it into your home. It might just be the last thing you do!' He winked at me theatrically and smiled. 'It's all academic, of course. There hasn't been a record of one for hundreds of years, if they ever existed, which is in some doubt. Why do you ask, my girl?'

'Oh, er...no...no reason. The fisherman, Dai, mentioned the word earlier, that's all. They found a survivor from the wreck last night. Apparently, that's the only word he'll say.'

Mr Gout's eyebrows rose. 'Really? How interesting. I shall have to pay the poor man a visit once he's feeling better. Probably nothing to it. You'll soon learn, living here, Clementine, my dear, that sailors can be a superstitious lot.' His eyes twinkled, and I forced myself to meet his smile before asking one last question.

'So they just bring good fortune, then? They don't...do other things?'

'Good fortune, yes. And warnings, as I say. Oh, and they help with the housework! That would be handy!' Mr Gout chuckled heartily and returned to his book, engrossed in seconds. My heart dropped. There was a clattering from the kitchen sink and I looked across to see Mrs Winchester frozen, her back still to the rest of the room, her shoulders a tight line. I said nothing.

That night, I lay awake once again. Could it be true? Or was I just being silly? Letting my imagination run away with me. It wouldn't be all

41

that surprising if I was getting carried away. I had been introduced to a poltergeist just two days before! Custard had tonight chosen to settle down on the rug beside me, between my mattress and the fire. He was fast asleep, his little chest going steadily up and down. Though why it should, as he hardly needed to breathe, I did not know. The room was bathed in his soft blue glow, his presence surprisingly comforting.

Then again, I reasoned, if ghost rabbits existed and could eat carrots, then maybe I *had* been followed from the station by a Klabautermann that first night. And if I had…then I'd led it straight to Oystercatcher Cottage.

It would explain the strange goings-on. And the presence I had felt out in the woodshed. But if it was true, then I had brought great danger to my new employer's house. Would Mr Gout forgive me? I wondered. Or cast me out. He seemed like such a jolly soul, but I had glimpsed a harder side to him that evening. Could he forgive the misfortune I might have brought to his door?

'Oh, enough of this!' I muttered to myself, throwing back the blanket and sitting up. Sleep would never come at this rate, and I needed to know for sure. I'd done nothing of use since arriving in Abermywl, so let this be the first thing. I would investigate the woodshed. Find out if something lurked in its impenetrable shadows, or if I was just a frightened, homesick little girl.

I clambered to my feet, careful not to wake

the sleeping Custard, lit a small candle and quietly made my way outside. The cold bit at my exposed arms and legs and I wished I'd thought to change out of my nightdress. When I saw the woodshed, an inanimate beast slumbering in the darkness, I considered going back to bed and waiting till daylight. But no. I had to know.

I advanced on the gaping doorway, holding my guttering candle out in front of me like a talisman. Its weak light faded to insignificance in the face of the building's forbidding internal shadows. I inched closer, poking my head inside.

'Hello? Is there anybody there?'

Silence was my only reply.

I moved in further, raising the candle above my head, straining my eyes to catch any flash of movement, my ears for the sound of pattering feet. But I saw nothing but wood, heard nothing but the barest whisper of the wind.

I'd been wrong, it seemed. The woodshed was devoid of life (unless you counted spiders, of which there were many), filled only with loosely stacked logs. I breathed a little sigh of relief, but quickly felt the burning shame of letting my imagination get the better of me. I returned to the house, closing the back door quietly behind me and blowing out the candle.

There was something sitting on the kitchen table.

Lit by the ghostly light of the sleeping Custard, I could make out a creature about the size of a small child perched on the edge of the table, swinging its stubby legs over the edge. It wore little black leather wellington boots, thick waxed waders, and a patched cable-knit jumper under an over-large raincoat, rolled up at the sleeves. Perched on its head was a yellow sailor's cap. I looked into large, round eyes the colour of tea leaves and felt the breath catch in my throat.

The creature observed me for some moments, then quite unconcernedly produced a carved wooden pipe and said, 'I don't suppose you have a spot of tobacco about your person? Mine's all damp.' Its voice put me in mind of a frog, as did its face; dark lumpy skin, flat nose, and wide, thick lips like glistening slugs.

'I...I'm afraid I don't smoke,' I said at last, feeling faintly ridiculous. The smell of the salt marsh came off the creature in waves as it moved.

It rolled its enormous eyes. 'Of course you don't.'

When I didn't reply, it added, 'I've cleaned the oven, by the way. You're welcome.'

'Um...thank you. I hope it's not rude to ask, but, are you a Klabautermann?'

'And if it *were* rude to ask?' it said, tapping its pipe experimentally on the table and brushing away the few damp particles that fell out.

'Then I should be very sorry for it.'

'And that would make it better, would it? You being sorry?'

'I hope so.'

'I see,' said the creature, pocketing the pipe and getting to its feet on the tabletop. 'Well, luckily for you, it ain't rude and no, I ain't a Klabautermann.'

'Oh,' I said, a little confused. 'But I thought–'

'I *used* to be a Klabautermann. Only now I've lost my ship, so I don't really know what I am. Just a plain old Kobold, I suppose, or Cofgod in the old English, if you prefer...' it said, in a passable imitation of Mr Gout.

'You heard that?'

'I was nearby. And I ain't never murdered nobody! You ask anyone. There's been a few accidents over the years, but ain't nobody gonna blame me for them! But never mind that. The name's Klous. What's for dinner?'

'I'm sorry?' I asked, trying to keep up with the bizarre conversation.

'I'm starving!' Klous said. 'I suppose it would be too much to hope you might have a little pease pudding? My favourite, that is. Right lovely with a little boiled pork.'

'I...I'm not sure. Mrs Winchester doesn't like me interfering in the kitchen, I'm afraid.'

'That the grumpy one? Face like a prune what's been sitting on the shelf too long?' Klous said.

I nodded, feeling a little guilty, but it was an apt description. 'I'd be happy to make you some if we have the ingredients.'

It seemed a good idea to appease the thing until I could figure out exactly what I was dealing with.

Klous's face broke into a grin, revealing a set of pointy yellow teeth. 'I knew I liked you,' he said. 'That would be proper kind of you, that would. Nice to see there's still a little goodness in the world. It brings a tear to my eye, really it does.'

'Only if we have any split peas,' I warned.

As it turned out, we did. I found a couple of onions in a cupboard, and thyme and bay in the front garden, so set to work lighting the cold stove from the fire's embers. 'I'm afraid it could take a while,' I said. 'Would you like a cup of tea while you wait?'

'One in a million you are, miss,' Klous said, investigating his ear with a claw-like fingernail. 'One in a million.'

As the fire caught and I busied myself filling a kettle for tea and a pan for the pudding, the little Klous looked around the room with interest, humming a sea shanty. I thought desperately of what I should say next. Despite Mr Gout's warnings, the Kobold didn't seem all that dangerous. In fact, I found I quite liked him. 'Thank you for fixing the cupboards. And for smoking the fish.'

'S'alright,' said Klous happily. 'I'm good at stuff like that.'

'Well, it's really very kind of you. I just wondered...well, I wondered why? Why did you come here, I mean?'

But before Klous could answer there came a loud 'Ah-ha!' from the other side of the room. I turned to see Mrs Winchester, standing in her bed-clothes, clutching the ends of a shawl to her chest with a bony hand, and glaring at me with a look of grim triumph. 'Caught in the act! I knew you were up to no–' the sentence died in her throat as she took in Klous, still standing on the table.

'Wotcha, Grandma,' he said, doffing his cap to her.

Mrs Winchester made a strange gurgling sound. 'What have you done? What have you let into this house!'

'Um…Mrs Winchester, this is Klous. He's a Klabautermann, or rather he was. Now he's not sure what he is…except hungry. So I offered to make him some pease pudding. I hope that's alright.'

She goggled at me. 'Alright? *Alright*? Of course it's not alright! Don't feed the disgusting thing or we'll never be rid of it!'

Klous bridled. 'Oh, right nice that is! And after I've come all this way n'all! I've a good mind to–'

But he was distracted. All the noise seemed to have roused Custard from his slumber, and upon seeing a stranger in his kitchen – and to be fair, they came little stranger than Klous – the ghostly rabbit had launched himself from floor to chair to table and was now spiritedly nipping at the Kobold's ankles. Klous tried to nudge him away with a foot that passed straight through. 'What's this?' he said.

'That's just Custard. He's a poltergeist. I'm afraid he's a little excitable,' I said weakly.

'A rabbit poltergeist? Now I've seen everything. What's it doing?'

'Something useful for once!' Mrs Winchester cried, grabbing a broom from where it stood in the corner and brandishing it in front of her like a lance. 'Begone with you, you horrible creature!'

Klous grabbed the end of the broom and yanked it out of her hands with surprising strength. 'Right!' he said with a croak. 'I've had just about enough of this!'

'Um, perhaps I should just go and wake Mr Gout,' I said.

'You'll do no such thing. Mr Gout is an important man and I don't want him bothered with your nonsense in the middle of the night!' said Mrs Winchester. 'This is your mess, and now I'm going to clear it up! Because. That's. My. Job!' She punctuated the last four words by throwing anything she could get her hands on at the unfortunate Klous. A book, two apples and an ornamental boot scraper flew across the room, the last narrowly missing the Kobold and taking a chunk out of the table's surface.

'Right!' hissed Klous, springing through the air – looking more frog-like than ever – and landing on a little bookcase, which toppled over. He leapt again, this time coming down on a vase of flowers, which he kicked to the floor with a vicious grin.

'You little toad!' Mrs Winchester shrieked. She reclaimed the broom and began running after the airborne Kobold, who bounced from surface to surface, knocking down whatever he could reach. Custard, now thoroughly overexcited, zipped around the room after them. It was at this point the kettle began a high-pitched whistle, and I put my hands to my head in horror at the chaos now consuming Oystercatcher Cottage.

Then there was an almighty bang and Mr Gout

burst through the back door, an imposing sight in a striped nightdress under a green silk dressing gown. His blond hair stuck up in a variety of angles and his feet were quite bare. He had obviously arrived from outside the house, and travelled in a hurry, because his feet were liberally coated with thick brown mud that splashed up his exposed calves. His eyes travelled the room, taking in the scene before him. Then, quite calmly, he said, 'Mrs Winchester, kindly put down that broom, there's a good woman. Miss Trussel, if you would be so good as to take that kettle off the heat? I believe it's trying to tell you it's ready. Now then, who do we have here?'

He levelled his eyes at Klous, who, to my great surprise, actually lowered the candlestick he had been about to throw through the window, looking guilty.

'Why don't we all sit down with a nice cup of tea and have a little chat, hmm?' said Mr Gout.

'I was promised pease pudding,' Klous muttered, pouting like a child.

Mr Gout raised an eyebrow. 'Really? At this time of night? How delightfully unconventional. A splendid idea!'

PART FOUR

And so, in the dark of the night, with half the contents of Oystercatcher Cottage lying broken on the floor at our feet, we sat down to tea while the split peas boiled, the smell of the herbs rising into the room on the steam. Mrs Winchester glowered across the table at me. I tried not to meet her eyes.

'Well now, this is much more civilised,' said Mr Gout, taking a gulp of his tea and smacking his lips. 'So…who wants to tell me what's going on?'

Before I could get in a word, Mrs Winchester was talking.

'Miss Trussel has brought disaster on this house, that's what's going on! She led a demon to our very door, then, to make matters worse, she invited it inside!'

'I ain't no demon, Granny,' said Klous, sticking his amphibian nose in the air. 'You wanna get your facts straight. Slander, that is!'

The housekeeper scoffed, and Klous's bulbous eyes narrowed.

'That's not exactly what happened,' I said, and tried to explain, to the best of my ability, what little I knew. When I had finished, Mr Gout stroked his chin, which was speckled with stubble for the first time since I had met him, and fixed Klous with an enquiring gaze.

'Perhaps you might tell us what brings you to our little home?' he asked. 'Pure chance? Or something more?'

But Klous was still eyeing Mrs Winchester with great distaste. 'Not sure I wanna say,' he said. 'Not sure some people here are showing me the proper respect. I want an apology.'

Mrs Winchester choked. 'Me? Apologise? Outrageous!'

'I could bring this house down around your ears, you old crone!'

'I'll not sit here and be insulted!'

'The only reason this cottage isn't a smoking hole in the ground already is the girl,' Klous said, turning to Mr Gout with an evil grin. 'You ought to kick the old baggage out. Past her usefulness, I reckon.'

Mrs Winchester rose to her feet and pointed a bony finger at the Kobold. 'Now look here, you slimy little–'

'I think it might be best if you were to let us chat alone, my dear,' Mr Gout cut in.

The housekeeper's face was stony. 'Very well. Come on, girl, we can–'

'I shall require Miss Trussel to stay here,' Mr Gout said. 'She is, after all, my apprentice.'

The blood drained from Mrs Winchester's face. She stood like a statue, staring at Mr Gout, her mouth a tight pressed line. Eventually, she blinked. 'I see. Well, excuse me, I'm sure. I shouldn't want to be in the way. I'll just go to bed then.'

She left the room without another word, the door to her bedroom slamming in the silence she left in her wake. Klous smirked after her.

'Now then, let us try again. How did you come to be here, my friend?' Mr Gout asked the Kobold. 'What happened to your ship?'

Klous bared his pointy teeth. 'I sank it,' he croaked.

'What!' I said, horrified. 'But people died in that wreck! You told me you'd never murdered anyone!'

Mr Gout held a hand up for silence. Klous made a little harrumph, although it sounded for all the world like a ribbit. 'All right, all right, keep your knickers on! They was all already dead, weren't they.'

Mr Gout leant forward keenly. 'The crew were dead before the ship sank?'

'That's what I said, ain't it? What sort of monster do you think I am? Dead as doornails, the lot of 'em. Cursed.'

'Cursed? That is ill news indeed. You are sure?'

'Course I'm sure! It was my ship. You think I don't know what's going on onboard my own ship? Point of pride, that is, for us Klabautermann.'

'My apologies,' said Mr Gout. 'You have me at a disadvantage. I must confess you're the first of your kind I have had the pleasure of meeting. I am not familiar with your ways. The old texts can be... unreliable.'

'Unreliable? More like bleedin' libel, if you ask me,' Klous said, his long, thin nostrils flaring. 'But you're not to blame, sir. Not many of us about no more. This modern world don't belong to us.'

'Indeed. But to get back to this curse...'

Klous's warty forehead furrowed. 'Must have been a curse,' he muttered, and I thought I saw a haunted look swim into his round eyes, before he blinked and stared back at us defiantly. 'Took 'em all. Every one of 'em. One day, everything was normal, the next...poof. It spread like a sickness. Took the captain first. Then the first mate. Half a dozen sailors after that. Inside three days, the entire crew was dead and there wasn't a thing I could do to help 'em.'

'All but one,' I said.

Klous's head whipped round to face me. 'What's that?'

'They found a survivor. They pulled him out of the water last night. He's not in a good way, though. That's how I knew you were a Klabautermann. Apparently, it's the only word he'll say.'

I'd thought the little creature would be pleased, but Klous looked horrified. 'There *were* no survivors.'

'This curse,' Mr Gout said, leaning forward over the table, a crease running down his brow. 'What exactly were the symptoms?'

'It burnt through the crew like a fever,' Klous said. 'Only there wasn't nothing that would put it out. It started with nothing more than a stiff neck–'

'Dai!' I cried, my hands flying to my mouth

with the horrible realisation. 'He was with the man they pulled from the sea last night and he was complaining of a sore neck when we saw him this morning!'

Klous flopped back against his chair, his face ashen. 'Then I have failed. The curse has made it to shore.'

Mr Gout got to his feet, his face as serious as I had ever seen it. 'We must see to this at once. Miss Trussel, kindly alert Mrs Winchester that I need to see her right away, then be ready to leave the house in five minutes. We must hurry.'

'You can't stop it,' Klous said, shaking his head. 'I couldn't stop it.'

'We must try,' Mr Gout said. 'Clementine, go now!'

I shot to my feet and all but ran from the room. I opened the door to Mrs Winchester's bedroom without knocking and opened my mouth to call out – then stopped.

The room was empty; the window hanging open. Mrs Winchester was gone.

The disappearance of his housekeeper seemed to agitate Mr Gout even more than the prospect of a deadly curse loose in the village.

'I just can't understand it,' he kept saying. 'This isn't like her at all!'

I said nothing.

The two of us were hurrying down the hill towards Dai's house. We had to ascertain if the fisherman really was afflicted, or just suffering from a strained neck. Klous bounded along at our side in great leaps to keep up.

'You don't want me with you. The sight of me tends to give people the willies!' he said. He'd wanted to stay out of sight back at Oystercatcher Cottage, but Mr Gout had insisted he join us.

'We might need your magic, or your expertise. You're the only one who's seen this curse before.'

Klous had relented, but the little creature was clearly unhappy being out in the open.

It was a clearer night than the one of my arrival in Abermywl, and our path down to the cottage by the train station was well lit by the moon. It was still cold, though, and I shivered as Mr Gout hammered his large fist against the fisherman's wooden door. Klous leapt into the hedge across the road and skulked in the shadows.

'Mr Thomas?' Mr Gout called out. 'Dai? It's Theophilius.'

All seemed dark within, but the door was answered with surprising speed. However, it wasn't Dai who appeared, but Gruffydd Pew, looking grey and drawn in the silver light. He leaned heavily against the doorframe, but still managed to look us up and down with dislike.

'What do you two want?'

'We have come to check on Mr Thomas,' said Mr Gout.

'At this time of night? He's fine.'

'I have reason to believe otherwise.'

Mr Pew looked shifty. 'Listen, mister, we look

after our own around here, alright? We don't need no outsiders–'

'Gruffydd, do not test me. Time is of the essence.' Mr Gout did not actually move, at least not that I could tell, but he suddenly seemed to loom larger next to me. Mr Pew must have felt it as well, because he shied back from the doorway. He did not, however, move aside.

'I've already sent for the doctor.'

'The good doctor will not be able to help. But I might. If I'm right, Dai will not last the night without my intervention, and by the look of it, neither will you.'

This did the trick. Mr Pew paled even further and stumbled out of the way to allow us entry.

The house was in complete darkness, but we found Dai in the first room we entered, slumped in a chair, practically hugging the stove. He looked even worse than Mr Pew, as though he had wasted away in the hours since I had last seen him. The fisherman was shivering uncontrollably, and I could hear his teeth chattering from the doorway. He didn't acknowledge our arrival.

'Get some light in here,' Mr Gout said to me. 'Then see if you can't coax some more heat out of that stove.'

I hurried to obey as he knelt down with a grunt beside the man in the chair and took his hand gently in his own. 'Dai, it's Theophilius. Can you tell me what happened, old chap?'

The fisherman's sunken eyes opened slowly. His

breathing was fast and shallow. 'Mr Gout, sir?' His voice was little more than a whisper. I hurried over with a candle I'd managed to light.

'I'm here,' said Mr Gout.

I set about trying to stoke up the stove while Mr Gout examined Dai. By the time I had a healthy flame going, my master had inspected the fisherman's eyes, taken his pulse, listened to his heart, listened to his belly, scraped the fur from his tongue, and looked intently at what was under the man's fingernails. Finally, he produced his trusty leather notebook and thumbed through the age-worn pages, scratching his chin and mumbling under his breath.

'I don't suppose you keep newt livers in your kitchen, do you?' he asked the almost insensible Mr Thomas. The man did not respond, but Mr Gout shook his head anyway. 'No, too much to hope for, really, at this time of year. We will have to think around the problem. Clementine, my dear, would you be so good as to search our fine friends' cupboards for horseradish?'

I did as I was bid, rifling through the practically empty kitchen cupboards, all the while wondering how on earth horseradish was supposed to cure a magical curse strong enough to wipe out an entire ship. I never got to find out, because my search came up empty. Mr Thomas really had disturbingly bare cupboards.

'He hasn't got any,' I said.

Mr Gout made a face. 'Blast! Well, what have we

got to work with?'

I held out the only foodstuffs my search had revealed. 'A half-empty jar of pickled eggs. Sorry.'

'Now, now. Half *full*, surely, my dear girl. Let us remain positive. Hand it over.'

I passed him the sorry-looking jar, and he scrutinised it, then shrugged his round shoulders. 'Not ideal, but it will have to do.' He unscrewed the rusted top and knelt down next to Dai. The fisherman recoiled at the smell of the vinegar, turning even paler.

'Chin up, old boy!' Mr Gout said with a broad smile. 'Soon have you feeling bouncier than a spring lamb in the sunshine. Now, I'll not lie to you; this will most likely be unpleasant. But it's all for the greater good. Bottoms up!' And with a swift motion, he brought the jar and its eye-watering contents to the fisherman's lips, and tilted back his head.

Poor Dai probably took on three mouthfuls before his feeble body registered what was going on. Mr Gout got to his feet and stepped back in one fluid motion as the unfortunate Mr Thomas choked and gagged, then vomited noisily onto the flagstone floor. Mr Gout looked at the mess and grimaced. 'Ah. In retrospect, I probably should have found a bowl or something first.'

'Was that supposed to help?' I asked.

'Oh, certainly,' he said, stepping back carefully as the puddle on the floor threatened the toe of his shoe. 'If there is one thing in this world that I have learnt, Miss Trussel, it is that there was never a truer sentence spoken in the great English tongue than "Better out than in."'

Indeed, despite my scepticism, I had to admit that once he was suitably recovered, Dai did seem to have a little more colour in his cheeks than he'd had before.

At length, Klous appeared in the kitchen doorway. He eyed the barely conscious Dai warily and silently beckoned me over. I went to him and found Mr Pew, who I had quite forgotten, collapsed in the hall.

'This is it alright,' Klous said, shaking his head. 'This is the curse.'

I called for Mr Gout and between us we manoeuvred Mr Pew into a chair at the kitchen table.

'The curse is clearly already spreading,' said Mr Gout. 'We must act quickly or by daylight half the village will be infected.'

'But how do we stop it? Klous said he couldn't, so what can we do?' I asked. I needed no reminder of the stakes. It had already occurred to me that if Gruffydd had caught the curse from Dai, then we too must already be infected.

'I know little about Klabautermann magic,' Mr Gout admitted to Klous. 'But I am not surprised you were unable to break this particular spell. I had my suspicions from hearing your account of what happened to your unfortunate crew, but my examination of Mr Thomas has confirmed my fears. This is no ordinary curse. Fortunately, however, I'm something of an expert on curses.'

'So you think you'll be able to break it?' I asked, while Klous looked unconvinced.

'Perhaps,' said Mr Gout. 'Your average curse is usually little more than a simple hex: petty magic, worked by those with little true power. Many can cast them, with some knowledge and determination. But this...well, this is a whole different kettle of fish. Whoever cast this used a lot of power to do so. Magic of this kind is rare, as are those who can wield it. I suspect our best course of action is to track down the source of this curse. That so-called survivor seems the obvious suspect.'

He turned back to Dai, who had the slightest hint of a flush in his cheeks now and was watching us through half-open eyes. 'Where is he, Dai? This man you pulled from the water?'

It took Dai some time to speak. When he did, his voice was dry and faint. 'Gone. Disappeared. We brought him here to rest up. Then...then I started feeling all strange. I tried to stop him from leaving, but I was already too weak and he pushed me aside.'

'But his leg,' I said. 'Wasn't it broken?'

'Aye. I don't know how he even got out of bed!'

'How long ago was this?' Mr Gout asked.

Dai attempted a shrug. 'An hour? Two?'

The brief conversation had already tired him.

After administering the same pickled egg treatment to a weakly outraged Mr Pew, we left the two fishermen in the dismal little kitchen and headed back out into the night. I didn't like leaving them in that state, but there was little we could do for them by staying. The survivor was the key.

'How are we going to find him? He could be anywhere by now!' I said.

'Not anywhere,' said Mr Gout. 'If he is responsible for the curse, he will likely want to head where he can infect the maximum number of people.'

Klous gave a little snort. 'Then he jumped ship in the wrong town. I've seen graveyards livelier than Abermywl. No offence.'

Mr Gout was looking out into the darkness towards the town, scratching his chin thoughtfully, but he answered the little Klabautermann anyway. 'Oh none taken, dear chap. We like the quiet life here by the sea.'

He continued to stare out into the black, tapping his chin with his fingers and springing up and down on his heels. 'But,' he said at length, 'If there was a place I'd go looking for a little action, it would be The Ship and Cockle.'

'Really?' I said without thinking. I wouldn't have called the small room I'd sat in with Mrs Winchester that afternoon a hub of activity.

'Oh yes,' Mr Gout replied, his old sparkle returning to his eyes for a moment. 'Old Mal always did know how to run a good bar. And if you've never seen a fisherman drink, then you don't even know the meaning of the word.'

'That's true,' Klous agreed, nodding sagely.

'Yes, the pub is where our quarry will be heading alright. We should hurry.'

Without another word, he set off into the night.

I met Klous's round eyes, and he shrugged. We hurried to follow.

The high street was deserted when we reached it. The only sign of life was two seagulls pecking at what looked like an old fish head in the road. They gave us the evil eye as we approached, then launched themselves into the air, settling on the roof of a shop. The pub lay silent at the end of the street. A single light flickered through the glass of the windows. Not a sound issued from inside.

'Oh yes, quite the nightlife,' Klous muttered as he hopped along beside me. If Mr Gout heard the comment, he ignored it.

The waves lapped lazily against the jetty as we approached the pub. The door swung inwards with a creak at Mr Gout's touch.

'Careful now. We don't know what we might be walking into,' he said.

I took a deep breath and followed the other two inside.

At first I thought the place was empty. The solitary candle on the bar-top guttered in the air from the open door, producing only enough light to give real texture to the darkness. Then, as my eyes grew accustomed to the various shady shapes in front of me, I realised that what at first had looked like sacks were in fact the patrons, slumped, unmoving, over the tables.

'We're too late!' I said with a gasp.

'No.' Klous sniffed the stuffy air. 'They're alive.

For now. I can smell 'em.'

'Mal?' Mr Gout called softly. 'Mr Pottersburgh? You in here, old chap?'

There was a groan from somewhere across the room. Then a shaking hand appeared next to the candle on the bar-top, shortly followed by the head and shoulders of the barman. His face looked almost skeletal in the weak light. 'That you, Theo?' he croaked, hauling his upper body over the bar and clinging on with weak fingers.

'The very same,' said Mr Gout, hurrying through the hatch in the bar and helping the man properly to his feet. He half carried him to the nearest chair, and the publican sagged into it with relief. He looked almost as bad as Dai and Gruff.

'Well,' he said, smiling weakly. 'I thought maybe I'd undercooked the lamb in the cawl, but if you're here, I suspect I'm off the hook.' His face froze as he caught sight of Klous, who was prodding one of the slumped-over patrons with a clawed finger. 'Oh bugger, I'm dead. Is that a demon?'

The Klabautermann stopped his prodding and crossed his arms with a pout. 'Why does everyone keep saying that?'

'Don't worry, old chap, you're quite alive,' Mr Gout said reassuringly.

Mal leaned back in his chair and closed his eyes. 'Oh good. I'd hate to think being dead was this painful. What's going on, Theo?'

Mr Gout grasped the man by the shoulders 'Listen carefully, Mal. I need to know if you've seen the man they pulled from the sea. Has he been in here tonight?'

The publican gave a wheezing laugh that looked as if it might finish him off. He winced. 'Oh, I've seen him alright.'

'What happened, Mal? It's very important that you tell me; lives are at stake.'

Mal smiled again. 'Oh, you'll save the day, old friend. You always do.'

'What happened, Mal,' Mr Gout repeated.

The publican took a deep breath, then began to explain. 'It came in about an hour ago. Lurched through the doorway like something that crawled out of a grave.'

'*It*?' I said. 'You mean the survivor?'

The man shook his head. 'I'll take your word for it that I'm still alive, but there is no way that creature is among the living. Nothing that looks like that could still be drawing breath. Not to mention the smell. It pushed open the door, and I'd swear an icy chill swept in here ahead of it. Poor Mr Turnbridge damn near fainted at the sight of it. That's him, at the table by the door. Is he alright? Is everyone else alright?'

'For now, but time is of the essence, Mal,' Mr Gout said.

Mal managed a nod and continued. 'Well, it came in, dragging that broken leg behind it like a ball and chain. Then it just sort of stood there, right in the middle of the room, looking at everybody with those horrible blank eyes. Killed the mood, I can tell you that. Even put Farmer Gwilym off his pint.'

'What did it do then?' I asked.

Mal looked at me. 'Nothing.' he said. 'Absolutely nothing. Which is far more unnerving than it sounds. In the end I approached the thing and I said "Look here, pal, if you're not going to buy anything, you can sod off. We don't want any trouble."'

'And what did he say?' asked Mr Gout.

'*It*,' the publican insisted. 'Didn't say anything. Just turned its horrible face towards me, opened its mouth – which was an experience in itself, let me tell you – then sort of *breathed* at me.'

'It breathed at you?' I said, confused.

'It smelt like walking into the jaws of hell.' A shiver wracked Mal's body. 'Made me feel quite peculiar.'

'In what way, exactly?' Mr Gout pressed.

'Weak. I sort of stumbled away, back behind the bar. Then there was this pain in my neck, like I'd been sleeping funny, you know?'

'That fast?' Mr Gout said, more to himself, it seemed, than any of us. He stood up straight and stared out of the window thoughtfully.

'Mr Thomas' neck didn't start hurting until the morning after he pulled him...it, from the sea,' I said.

'It's getting stronger!' Klous said, jumping up onto a table and knocking over a half-drunk pint.

Mal tried to focus on the Klabautermann with bleary eyes, then grabbed my arm with a clammy hand. 'You can see that too, right?'

I nodded, patting his hand reassuringly. 'Don't worry, Klous is a friend.'

'Oh good, gooooood...' the publican slurred. He was looking more unwell by the second. 'I had a friend once. Well...I say friend...he was a bit of an arse, really. Had a visit from the Hobgoblins, didn't he, Theo?' At this he began to laugh wheezily, then soon descended into a violent coughing fit.

I turned to my master, who was still staring out of the window. 'I think he's hallucinating.'

'We need to find him, and fast,' Mr Gout said, turning from the window but ignoring me. 'Any idea where he went, Mal?'

The publican shook his head stiffly. 'No idea. But just ask Mrs Winchester.'

'Mrs Winchester was here?' I asked.

Mr Gout slapped a podgy hand to his forehead. 'Of course! I should have guessed this is where Angharad came. She always did like a drink after an argument.'

Mal coughed out a laugh, sinking slightly lower in his chair. 'Must have been quite the argument, the way she was knocking it back. Anyway, not long after I started to feel queer the rest of the room began toppling over, too. And the thing, this survivor of yours, just turned around like nothing had happened and walked back out the door. Then old Mrs Winchester, who'd been sitting in the corner the whole time, staggered to her feet and followed. I tried to go after her but...well, I think I must have passed out.'

'She followed it?' Mr Gout said, frowning.

Mal nodded. 'I don't know how she managed it. The rest of us could barely stand.'

'Oh, you know Angharad,' said Mr Gout with a grim, if slightly proud, smile. 'There's not much that will stop her once she sets her mind to something.'

'Even so, she can't have got far,' Mal said. 'But look, Theo, what exactly is going on? Are we sick or something? Do I need to be worried?'

'Not sick,' Mr Gout said. 'Cursed, I'm afraid. But don't worry, we'll get to the bottom of this, I promise.' He grimaced, then rubbed the back of his neck with a hand. The motion caught my attention, then made my heart sink as I realised something.

'Sir,' I whispered. 'My neck hurts.'

He locked eyes with mine. 'Yes, Miss Trussel, mine too, I'm afraid to say. We must hurry!'

'But how? How are we going to find the survivor? Even if Mrs Winchester is still with it, we have no way of contacting her.'

'Oh, I can find her,' Klous piped up, sniffing the air again. 'I'd be able to smell that old crone anywhere.'

'You can lead us to her?' Mr Gout asked. Then, when the little creature nodded, he asked, 'What about the survivor?'

Klous shook his head. 'It's weird, but I ain't getting anything off him, whoever he is. Tha's probably why I never found him on me ship. Something's protecting 'im.'

'Curious indeed,' Mr Gout said. 'But let us deal with the problem in front of us. We must find

Mrs Winchester and hope she can tell us more. But first, Mal, dear chap, I don't suppose you happen to have, anywhere in this fine establishment, some horseradish, or failing that, a nice jar of pickled eggs?'

PART FIVE

The wind had picked up since we'd entered the pub and it now tore at our clothes as we hurried back up the high street and then along the country lanes, following Klous, who would stop every few feet, sniff the air, then leap away again like a frog. The sound of the waves was our constant companion, the coast never far away. Mr Gout looked troubled.

'Why would Mrs Winchester risk herself like this? Why did she not simply come to me?'

I was silent for a moment, then spoke. 'She might have felt she couldn't. She doesn't seem happy with my presence here.'

The large man sighed, and his shoulders drooped. 'Perhaps. I just don't understand what she was thinking. I've told her a hundred times I have no intention of dismissing her from my service. I would never do such a thing!'

'Maybe she's scared of losing her home?'

Mr Gout looked shocked. 'Why on earth should she be afraid of that?'

'Well, if you were to dismiss her, she'd presumably have to leave Oystercatcher Cottage.'

Mr Gout looked more confused than ever at

this. 'Leave? What on earth for–' Then I watched his round face change as a realisation dawned. 'Ah. I fear I have been remiss in my explanations, Clementine, dear. You have things quite backwards. Oystercatcher Cottage belongs to Mrs Winchester. It is me, and you, of course, who are the guests.'

I was dumbfounded. 'But...but then why–' however, I was cut off by an urgent hiss from Klous.

'We're close!'

The Klabautermann slowed, no longer bouncing forward, but creeping carefully. I followed suit, as did Mr Gout, who sprang delicately from tip-toe to tip-toe and might have looked comical in different circumstances. Shelving his revelation for future examination, I realised with a jolt that we had arrived at the section of coast path I had previously visited with Mrs Winchester.

'They're heading for the bay.'

Mr Gout nodded agreement, his brow furrowed in confusion, which I shared. If the man was trying to make his escape, why had he not simply gone straight from the pub to the quay, mere feet away? There he might have found a boat of some kind, but the bay offered no means of escape.

The three of us must have made quite the sight, creeping along in the pale light of the moon. The bulbous form of Mr Gout, springing from foot to foot like a man of half his size, the tiny Klous, crawling now like a toad, and me, the thoroughly, boringly normal girl in the middle. Luckily, there was no one to see us, unless you counted the sheep, who watched warily from the fields that bordered the coast path.

We soon came out onto the cliffs and looked down into the bay below. At first I saw nothing but the sand and the rolling waves, which were growing more powerful by the minute. Wind buffeted tufts of grass that sprouted from snags in the rock this way and that, but otherwise the bay seemed still and empty.

A sound rose above the roar of the sea, a crunching, shifting sound, like a heavy wet bag hitting the shingle. I tensed, and felt my companions do the same, but for a moment longer still we saw nothing. Then a figure erupted from the deep dark below the cliffs to our left, staggering into the centre of the beach and what little light the moon provided. The figure moved strangely, jerking and shifting as though it were fighting something unseen. With a jolt and a gasp, I realised it wasn't a single figure at all, but two, entwined tightly together, each straining to gain the upper hand. As they fought, they twirled to face us and I glimpsed two faces in the silver light: one wrinkled and dark, the other pale and gaunt.

Next to me, Mr Gout gave a strangled cry and sprang to his feet. 'Angharad!'

Without looking back to see if we were following, he began scrambling down to the beach below, dislodging a hail of dirt and stone in his haste.

'Well...there goes the element of surprise,' Klous muttered at my side. 'Come on!'

He sprang after Mr Gout and I struggled to follow, slipping and grazing a hand on the sharp rocks as I hurried to keep up. I hit the sand awkwardly and fell to my knees as Mr Gout thundered across the shifting pebbles, his gait much heavier than his usual grace. When he reached the battling pair, he grabbed each by their clothes and tore them apart with what must have been a tremendous effort. Mrs Winchester fell to the sand looking spent, but the man, the survivor, merely staggered a few steps back, then spun and took off towards the sea, lurching on his broken leg.

Mrs Winchester, panting hard, raised herself up on one shaking arm and reached after the retreating figure as if she could grab a hold of him. 'Don't let 'im get away, you fool!'

I pulled myself to my feet. Klous stood close by, his froggy face turning this way and that in confusion. 'Let who get away?' he said.

I didn't know what he meant, for it was clear who Mrs Winchester was talking about. Indeed, Mr Gout, after a moment's hesitation where he looked as though he would drop to his knees at his housekeeper's side, tore after the man. I followed carefully, unsure of what I would actually do if I caught up.

The survivor by now had reached the shallows and was staggering into the waves as if he meant to walk through them to freedom. The water slowed his progress, however, and Mr Gout soon caught up. A particularly large wave reared up and slapped him in the thighs, making him stumble. It passed over the survivor, however, as though his feet were nailed to the seabed, barely causing him to waver. But it was enough, for Mr Gout soon righted himself and, with a lunge through the shallows, grabbed his opponent by the shirt collar and began hauling him back to shore.

At first the man kicked and struggled, but then he simply went limp, forcing Mr Gout to drag him across the sand like a corpse. He threw him down on the sand at our feet, releasing his grip on the man's collar, at which point the man sprang to life once more, rising to his feet with surprising speed. However, Mrs Winchester was ready for him. She launched herself at the stick-thin man and he toppled back to the sand once again, this time pinned by one hundred and twenty pounds of enraged housekeeper. But still he tried to rise. Mrs Winchester cursed as she fought to hold him.

'Well, don't just stand there, you great lummox! Help me!'

Mr Gout, drenched from the waist down, did as he was bid, kneeling in the sand and lending his not inconsiderable bulk to the process. The survivor thrashed and kicked his skinny legs, snarling and hissing like a wild animal, but to no avail. At length he fell still, although his eyes in their deep-set sockets roved wildly.

I hovered close by, unsure of how to help. Klous hopped from foot to foot agitatedly. 'Would someone mind telling me what is going on?' he said.

Mrs Winchester, still sprawled across her prisoner, shot him a filthy look. 'What does it look like?'

'It looks like you two fools are playing silly buggers in the sand while we're supposed to be catching the man who murdered my crew!'

'Well, seeing as I was sent away like a naughty schoolgirl, I've no idea what you're raving about,' Mrs Winchester said.

'The so-called survivor, you old crone!'

Mrs Winchester stared at him as though he were simple. 'Who do you think I'm lying on top of, you stupid toad?'

Klous looked blank. 'What?'

Mrs Winchester opened her mouth to speak again, but Mr Gout raised a hand to silence her, looking at the Klabautermann curiously. 'Tell me, Klous. Can you see anyone else on this beach apart from Miss Trussel, Mrs Winchester and myself?'

Klous looked more confused than ever. 'Of course not!'

Mr Gout, still lending his considerable weight to pinning the strange man to the floor, took on a deep, speculative expression. 'Fascinating! It would seem our friend here is warded from you, Klous. You can neither see nor hear him. It's no surprise now that you could not stop the spread of the curse on your ship. You wouldn't have even been able to detect what was spreading it.'

Klous looked stunned. He stared hard at the patch of sand beneath them where the survivor lay, pale and motionless, then reached out a tentative clawed finger, which connected with the prisoner's side and sent the Klabautermann leaping backwards in surprise. As the shock wore off, his amphibian face slid into an expression of grim realisation. 'Then that would mean...'

'Yes,' Mr Gout agreed with the unspoken thought. He regarded the man lying in the sand with a new dislike. 'The attack on your ship was well planned out. Whoever orchestrated it not only knew of your existence on the ship but also knew that you would be the one thing on board that would stand a chance of stopping the curse.'

'Speaking of the curse,' I said uneasily. 'Should we all be this close?'

'Oh, we are certainly already infected,' Mr Gout said. 'Which is why we need to have a strong word or two with our friend here,' he continued, shifting his weight, allowing Mrs Winchester to crawl aside so he could get a better look at the captive. The colour drained from his usually ruddy face. 'My word!'

'What is it?' I asked.

'Well, if I'm not too much mistaken, Clementine, my dear, it's a Zombie.'

Mrs Winchester, who had been crouching next to the prone man, scuffled back in alarm. 'It's a what?'

'A Zombie,' Mr Gout repeated. 'I confess I never thought to see one in the flesh. What with your sudden appearance in our lives, Klous, it's becoming quite the eventful evening, I must say!'

'You mean it's dead?' Mrs Winchester shivered,

and rubbed herself down with her hands, as though she could brush away the man's filth.

'In a manner of speaking, yes.' Mr Gout bent over the prone man to examine him more closely. The survivor gave no sign he was aware of his presence. He lay completely motionless, eyes open, staring at nothing.

'A Zombie, Miss Trussel, is a captured soul, trapped in its own deceased body and forced into servitude,' Mr Gout said, anticipating my question before I could voice it. 'It is said they originated in Haiti, with the practice of voodoo. However, I suspect that is not the origin of this particular specimen.'

'W...what makes you say that?' I asked, swallowing back my distaste as I looked down at the man's gaunt, expressionless face. Now that I got a good long look at him, it was quite easy to believe he was already dead. Nothing alive had eyes so devoid of any emotion.

'This,' said Mr Gout. And he reached for the sodden colour of the man's ragged shirt, twitching it aside to fully reveal an ugly scar on the man's collarbone that had been partially hidden.

I gave a gasp of recognition. Carved into the man's flesh was the familiar symbol of a single lily.

'It...it's the same...' I stammered.

'Yes,' Mr Gout agreed. 'It is the same symbol we found on the Alp that attacked your poor grandmother. Meaning the same dark power is behind this attack as well.'

'Speaking of,' broke in Mrs Winchester. 'How do we stop this curse you're on about? Do you know this thing incapacitated the entire Ship and Cockle in less than five minutes? Is that the curse? Because I'm far too busy to be dropping dead right now, thank you very much.' She did look exhausted. Now that the fight was over, she lay back in the sand, breathing hard and shallow, an unhealthy green tinge to her skin.

'How are you still standing?' I asked. I was already feeling pretty rough. The blood pounded in my ears and a cold sweat had broken out across my forehead. I rested my hands on my knees and breathed deeply.

'I ain't standing, I'm lying down,' she said. 'And I feel bloody awful.'

'Yes, but when we found the rest of the pub's patrons, they could barely move. How were you able to chase the...the Zombie all the way here?' I persisted.

The woman sniffed derisively. 'I keep telling everyone cold-water swimming is good for the constitution. Maybe now they'll believe me.'

'More to the point,' Mr Gout said, frowning. 'What were you thinking, running off after it on your own?'

Mrs Winchester gave him a furious look. 'I was thinking he was up to no good and getting away. Anyway, I was just following at first. He wasn't getting anywhere fast with that broken leg. But when it seemed like he was trying to make a break for it, I felt it prudent to act.'

'What was he planning to do, swim to freedom?' I asked.

'How should *I* know? Ask him, why don't you?' she snapped.

'Well, whatever his intention, the poor creature will have a hex bag about his person somewhere. We must find it. In order to break the curse, the bag must be neutralised.'

Mr Gout began to search through the Zombie's clothing. I hurried to help, feeling this was something I could manage. However, as I knelt down beside the still motionless body of the Zombie, its blank, grey eyes swivelled to look at me and I hesitated, a shiver running through my body.

'Can we not do something to help him?' I asked. 'Like we did for the Alp?'

Mr Gout paused in his search, looking thoughtful. 'It might be possible. But the hold over a Zombie by its master is much more direct than that of an Alp. They are motivated, not by pure instinct or hunger, but by the commands and will of their creator. It would take time and research, but yes, I would be hopeful of breaking that bond. We might even–'

But he was cut off abruptly as the man beneath him suddenly surged back to life, bringing his head up and smashing it into the unprepared face of Mr Gout, who fell back with a grunt. The Zombie was on his feet again before I could react.

'NO!' Mrs Winchester cried, flailing out in an attempt to stop the man, but missing. Klous tried his best, leaping at the spot where the Zombie had been, but clearly he could not see that the man was already loping across the sands back to the sea. Mr Gout lay on his back, stunned, as I struggled to my feet and tore after the source of the curse.

'The hex bag! He mustn't escape with the hex bag!' Mrs Winchester yelled after me.

The thing moved with a speed that still belied its frail appearance, and he once more reached the waves before I could intercept him. What he hoped to achieve by entering the water I could not guess, but with at least half the village now infected by the curse, there was too much at stake to allow any chance of his escape.

I urged my legs to greater speeds and splashed into the first waves, biting back the shock of the cold, forcing my body against the push of the water as I went deeper, following the Zombie that was already up to its waist. The waves were larger than they had been and I was closing my eyes against the spray that rose into my face each time they hit me. Soon, I too was waist deep, but by then, the Zombie was up to its chest. It didn't try to swim, however; it just kept putting one foot in front of the other, walking along the seafloor, until all too quickly its head disappeared under the surface of the water.

I felt a thrill of panic as I lost sight of the creature. The icy water lapped around my chest and my lungs froze. It was as though the weight of the sea was squeezing the air from my body and my breath came in short staccato bursts as I struggled to keep my footing. The Zombie did not resurface.

With a thrust of my feet, I dove beneath the water, flinging my arms out before me, even as I squeezed my eyes tightly shut, in the vain hope that I might reach my quarry. By some miracle, my fingers grazed wet fabric. A shirt? I grabbed a handful of the stuff, yanking it backward in an attempt to slow the Zombie, but instead I found myself drawn towards it, colliding with its bony body beneath the waves. I felt fingers like cold iron wrap around my arms, trying to drag me free, but I clung on for dear life with one hand, whilst the other searched the billowing folds of clothing for the hex bag.

My lungs ached . It was an impossible task. The cold of the water crept into my fingers and they scrabbled uselessly against my foe. Then, just as my lungs were about to burst and the Zombie succeeded in loosening my cramping hand, the other grasped something solid amongst the billowing folds of its clothing. My fingers were now too numb to make out what they held, but I tightened them around it with what little strength remained to me and allowed myself to be forced away from the creature until I hung in the empty water.

I had lost all sense of direction by this point, but as a fresh wave sent me spinning, I lashed out with my feet toward what I hoped was the surface. But there seemed no end to the water and my dress felt like a great weight, dragging me down. Panicking, my eyes flew open. I could see nothing in the water's murk, and the sting of the salt forced them to close again immediately. My legs kicked again, desperately now, my lungs screaming for air.

And then something grabbed me, hoisting my head clear of the water. I choked and wheezed and drew in great, painful lungs of air and sea spray, allowing myself to be manhandled into shallower water. My feet struck the seafloor, and I stumbled, nearly disappearing beneath the waves a second time. But my rescuer kept me upright. I dared to open my eyes again, blinking away the salt, sand and water that still ran from my drenched hair. The world swam in and out of focus as someone guided me through the shallows until finally, with great relief, I collapsed, shivering, on to the beach. The silhouette of my rescuer loomed over me and I blinked furiously to clear my vision. Eventually, a wrinkled face materialised.

'Well, my girl, that was a bloody stupid thing to do,' said Mrs Winchester. 'Brave. But bloody stupid. The curse not quick enough for you? You'd rather drown instead?'

'Is she alright? Clementine, my dear girl, you had us all frightfully worried!' came the voice of Mr Gout, somewhere to my left. My eyes still clearing, I turned to see him hurrying towards me, a handkerchief, stained red, clasped to his nose and little Klous in tow. In answer, I opened my hand, which still clutched tightly whatever I had prised away from the fleeing Zombie, and raised it aloft. It drew his eyes immediately. Abandoning his handkerchief and so revealing a red and swollen nose, he hurriedly snatched it from me.

'Miss Trussel, you really are a marvel!' he said, inspecting the item, which, now that I could see it clearly, appeared to be a small hessian package tied with black string. 'This is it! The hex bag!'

'You mean you can cure the curse now?' Klous asked, bouncing up and down to get a better look.

'I certainly have a chance, yes,' Mr Gout confirmed.

'But the Zombie got away,' I managed, my breath still coming sharply.

Mr Gout frowned. 'Yes. A pity. I had hoped to at least bring the poor thing peace.'

'Surely it won't survive out there?' asked Mrs Winchester, indicating the rolling waves with a flick of her arm. She was as soaked as I, the water dripping from her clothes making little dimples in the sand. I could see she was already sagging with the energy she had spent saving my life.

'Technically, it is already dead,' said Mr Gout. 'The sea will undoubtedly slow it down considerably, but it will make its way back to its master, eventually.'

'But w...why?' I managed, my body shaking. 'What was the point of all this?'

Klous was looking thoughtful. 'I think I've got the answer to that question.'

PART SIX

By the time we made it back to the cottage, I was feeling quite unwell. I was soaked, frozen, and my bones ached as though someone had a hold of each one and was stretching and twisting them violently. I could tell that Mr Gout and Mrs Winchester were feeling little better. The housekeeper, in particular, was struggling, and Mr Gout had to half support her for the last few minutes of our journey. The only one who seemed quite unaffected by the symptoms of the curse was Klous, who hopped anxiously around us, running ahead, then scampering back, like a dog with too much energy.

He'd argued for Mr Gout to attempt whatever he was going to try with the hex bag back on the beach. But Mr Gout had insisted we return, claiming it was vital he had access to his study. Now it was the little Klabautermann who pushed open the door to Oystercatcher Cottage, allowing my master to help Mrs Winchester over the threshold. I staggered after them.

'We must hurry,' Mr Gout said with a grunt, as he lowered the almost insensible Mrs Winchester into the comfy chair by the still smouldering fire. Custard had been sleeping on the rug but had awoken at our entrance. Clearly, the ghostly rabbit could tell something was wrong. He hopped agitatedly around Mr Gout's feet, clawing at his trousers until, with an effort, Mr Gout bent down and scooped the beast up in his arms.

'I think it's about time we had a taste of our own medicine. Clementine, would you be so good as to fetch the jar of pickled eggs you'll find in the left-hand kitchen cupboard?'

I made to comply, but Klous beat me to it, springing up to the cupboard and back before I'd moved more than a few paces. I took it from him with a weak smile.

'No newts' livers?'

Mr Gout made a face. 'Like I said before, wrong time of year.'

I unscrewed the lid to the jar of eggs and winced at the sharp smell. 'Do we have to? What does it do, exactly?'

'Purges the stomach, my dear. A little temporary relief. It will help, I promise.'

I staggered to the sink, then, holding my nose, I took a large, burning gulp of the vinegar. The effects were almost instantaneous, and I shall be forever grateful that my companions had the decency to turn their backs whilst what felt like every meal I'd eaten for the past year exited my body. But Mr Gout had been right: I did feel a little stronger afterwards.

He took the jar next and I faced the far wall, pretending not to hear as a series of indescribable sounds followed. Eventually they stopped, and I turned to see Mr Gout passing the pickled eggs back to Klous.

'We have to get to my study without delay,' he said, wiping his mouth and turning to me.

My head was swimming, which is perhaps why I snapped back my response to him, uncharacteristically sharp. 'Well, it would help if I knew where that was?'

He stared at me for a moment, one hand absentmindedly stroking the glowing Custard.

'I…I'm sorry, sir. I didn't mean to–'

'No, no, my dear girl. You are quite right,' he said. 'I'm afraid I haven't been a wonderful teacher so far, have I? And an even worse host! Please come with me. Klous, I wonder if I could press you to stay here and help Mrs Winchester with her medicine?'

The housekeeper was slumped in the chair where Mr Gout had dropped her. She appeared to have slipped into unconsciousness.

Klous' round eyes bulged and he fingered the jar nervously. 'Just hurry!'

Mr Gout simply nodded, then beckoned me to follow him. I did so out of the back door, past the woodshed, and then climbed the bank behind the house in his wake. It was not particularly steep, but my body moved as though I were walking through dough and I almost fell several times. I struggled on, doing my best to keep up, realising as I did so that dawn was already pushing back the veil of night.

As we crested the rise, I had to stop for a moment

to take in what I was seeing. Before us lay a view out across the bay that surpassed anything I had seen so far. Grey sand stretched out far below in a wide curve, cut off toward the horizon by more of the stark cliffs. They looked as though someone had taken a giant cake knife to the coastline. The sea rushed in to fill the void; a rippling plane of green, blue, black and grey. I could hear the waves from here, smell the salt on the wind, and the slight mist of rain that came with it felt like sea spray on my skin though the water was too far below us.

Just over the top of the hill, an old wheeled shepherd's hut was parked. The paint was faded and flaking, and the grass grew up around the wheels in great tufts, showing it had been there for some time. A thin stream of wood smoke rose from the crooked metal chimney.

Mr Gout was already at the door and he opened it, ushering me into the tiny room inside, which was filled with books. They spilled out of shelves, stood in large stacks on the wooden floor, and lay open across the small bench and table. A little round window shared the view out across the bay and an oil lamp stood unlit in one corner.

'This is your office?' I asked.

'Office, bedroom…whatever I need it to be. Mrs Winchester has Oystercatcher Cottage, I have my hut. We make do.' Mr Gout was panting now, sweat shining on his cheeks and forehead.

'But…don't you have a proper house?' I asked, struggling to understand. 'I mean, you always seem so…what I mean is, you don't look poor. Sorry, that was rude…'

'It's quite alright, my dear. I know my situation is…a little unorthodox. The truth is, I do have another house…somewhere.'

'Somewhere?'

'I lost it,' Mr Gout said with a shrug, then shot me a grin. 'I did say I was an expert on curses. Anyway, Mrs Winchester was kind enough to take me in, and we struggle through.'

I gaped at him. 'Are you saying you were cursed into forgetting where your own house is?'

Mr Gout nodded, gently placing Custard onto the table. The rabbit's blue glow lit the entire caravan in a pale wash of light. Mr Gout picked some books up off the bench and moved them aside so he could sit down at the table. I followed suit, sitting opposite him. Custard hopped across the table to sniff at my hand and I stroked his head, which made my fingers tingle.

'But then why not sleep in the cottage? Why come up here?'

'Ah, well, the curse also prevents me from sleeping under a proper roof.' He pointed at the caravan's ceiling with a sausage-like finger. 'This one's made of canvas, see? It's an annoying inconvenience, but I suppose I've become used to it after all these years.'

My mind reeled. 'But…but…you stayed at the Inn in Fairsop! The Golden Fleece, remember?'

He grimaced. 'Actually, I slept in the stable. Quite

comfy if you stack the straw just right. And horses, I find, are always welcoming to a roommate with a pocket full of carrots.'

I stared at him, opening and shutting my mouth a few times, unable to think what to say. He reached out and patted my hand. 'It's alright, my dear. I survive. But, as thrilling as examining the foolishness of my youth would be, we have a rather more urgent curse to attend to.'

'Of course; sorry,' I said, shaking myself, then rubbing my fingers hard into my tired eyes. I could have slept right there on the bench.

Mr Gout fished the sodden hex bag out of his pocket and began fiddling with the bindings. Soon he had it opened up on the table. Together, we examined the contents.

'I can't even make out what half of this stuff is,' I said. I held Custard back with one hand and reached out a finger to poke at the little pile with the other. Mr Gout quickly swatted it away.

'Don't touch it. I really couldn't say what the result would be.' He reached back into his jacket pocket and produced his leather notebook. It, too, was looking a little worse for the trip to the cove. Mr Gout opened it anyway, flicking through the pages, looking down at the hex bag, then back up to the scrawling notes and pictures that filled every page of the book.

While he worked, I looked again at the mixture of objects on the table. There were several of what appeared to be bones. Thankfully, they looked far too small to be human. Bird, perhaps. Then there was a lump of what I thought might be seaweed, but it looked black and brittle, despite its recent submersion. The rest of the hex bag's contents I could not begin to identify, apart from a tarnished silver coin of a denomination I did not recognise. Mr Gout continued to peruse his notes, muttering under his breath, shaking his head every now and again. Slowly, I felt my eyelids close.

I awoke some time later with a start. I was still sitting at the caravan table. Mr Gout stood by my side, his large hand on my shoulder.

'Terribly sorry to wake you, dear girl,' he said with a smile. 'But I didn't think you'd want to miss this part.'

Flustered, I tried to stand, hitting the front of my thighs on the underside of the table and sitting back down with a bump. Mr Gout held out a palm.

'No, no, stay seated, Clementine, my dear. It's been a trying night. Let us put an end to it.'

'You've found a way to end the curse?' I said through a yawn. I focused my eyes on my master's face. He looked dreadful. His skin was pale and waxen, his eyes dull and sunken. I felt no better. I couldn't imagine how he had even stayed awake, but he beamed down at me.

'I did!' he said. 'Not actually all that complex, once I had my head around the problem. We just need to burn the hex bag.'

'That's it?' I said, a little disappointed.

It must have shown on my face because Mr Gout laughed, then said, 'That's it. Well, almost. I've added one or two special things to the stove, to help matters along.'

I looked and noticed that the window to the little wood stove in the corner was now open, and the fire blazing merrily, whereas before it had barely been smouldering. I couldn't feel its heat, though. My clothes were still wet, and I felt as though I were still deep under the waves. I shivered uncontrollably.

Mr Gout coughed. 'Yes, best get on with it.'

He leaned over the table and carefully bundled the hex bag back together, then approached the fire.

'Hold on to your hats!' he said with a weary grin. Then he unceremoniously threw the little package into the flames, slamming the stove door closed. He backed away from the fire, retaking his seat at the table.

I watched the flames intently, but nothing happened.

'Did it work?'

'I think so,' he said, yawning and stretching his limbs experimentally. 'Why yes, I do believe I'm feeling a little better already.'

He was right, I realised. I too felt a little warmer, a little less dead tired.

'So that's it?'

Mr Gout smiled. 'That's it.'

'I must admit, I'm a little disappointed,' I said. 'I was expecting...well, I don't know what I was expecting, but something.'

Mr Gout yawned again, getting back to his feet. 'You'll find, my dear, that proper magic, powerful magic, rarely wastes effort on theatrics. But it is almost over. We will wait a few minutes to make sure, but then we should check on Mrs Winchester and the rest of the village.'

Covering my mouth, I stifled a half-yawn, half-groan. I really could feel the effects of the curse lifting, but we had still been up most of the night. I fought the urge to go back to sleep, watching Custard, who was sniffing at the blazing stove, his little nose twitching furiously. It made me smile, until the rabbit turned, yipping excitedly, and I realised he was trying to tell us something.

'What does he want?'

Mr Gout yawned. His eyes were barely open. 'Feeding, probably.'

'But he's dead.'

'Force of habit, I expect.'

I sniffed. 'Can you smell…flowers?'

I saw Mr Gout's nostrils flare, then his eyes snapped open wide. 'Lilies,' he said. 'I can smell lilies.'

By this time, Custard was hopping up and down, still yipping and obviously distressed.

'Up!' Mr Gout bellowed, lurching to his feet. 'Get up!'

I rose. 'What's happening?'

He grabbed me by the collar and practically threw me towards the door. 'Run!'

Staggering towards the door, I got it open. I

turned to ask again what was happening, but Mr Gout was right behind me and pushed me through. I fell down the steps into the morning light, landing on the grass, then felt myself being lifted by his firm hands.

We were only a few paces down the hill when there was an ear-splitting bang and a wave of heat knocked us both from our feet. I landed face first, back in the grass. When I rolled over and looked back, I saw the caravan was now a raging inferno of bright green flame. The wood stove door had half buried itself in the ground, just a couple of feet from my head.

Mr Gout lay next to me, propping himself up on his elbows and looking back at what remained of his home.

'Ah,' he said. 'A booby trap, if I'm not mistaken. Fascinating.'

'Your house!' I cried over the roar of the flame. 'All your books!'

'Yes, that is a little annoying,' he admitted. 'Still, better singed pages than fingers. Are you alright, Miss Trussel?'

'I...I'm fine.' I said, amazed at his calm. 'Shouldn't we try to put it out?'

Mr Gout made a face. 'Do you know, dear girl, I find I really can't be bothered.'

So we lay there, side by side, as the caravan burned.

After a minute, a blue light appeared out of the flames and Custard came hopping towards us.

'Custard, my friend! We owe you our lives!' Mr Gout greeted the rabbit, reaching out and ruffling the fur between his ears. 'How clever you are, to already be dead, and so avoid a most unfortunate accident.'

'Theophilius Gout! What have you done now, you ridiculous man?'

The shout drifted up to us from the cottage below. Mr Gout beamed at me.

'And it would seem Mrs Winchester is feeling much better, too. Splendid. Simply splendid. I say, my dear, could see your way to helping an old man to his feet? I fear I may have done myself a mischief.'

That afternoon found all four of us sat on a bench outside The Ship and Cockle, watching as the steady pace of coastal life reasserted itself around us. People seemed to have bounced back from the effects of the mysterious curse with surprising speed. Indeed, when Mr Thomas and Mr Pew passed us, Dai waved cheerily. Gruff pretended not to see us and slouched by with bad grace. Klous too looked a little uncomfortable. Indeed, he had lurked in the shadows behind the bench for some time before Mr Gout had convinced him to sit on it, though he earned little more than a few surprised glances from the populace of Abermywl.

'Many things have washed up here over the years. You, my friend, are far from the strangest,' Mr Gout explained.

'Tell me again about this lily?' Klous said, eyeing

suspiciously a fishwife who was coming out of the opposite shop.

'It is the sigil of whomever, or whatever, was responsible for all of this. The creator of the curse, and its Zombie dispersal system. They are responsible for the death of your crew,' said Mr Gout. He was dunking a piece of crusty bread in a bowl of cawl – which I had learnt was a sort of lamb stew. The juices ran down his fingers and he licked at them appreciatively.

'But you have no idea who they are?'

Mr Gout picked something out of his teeth with a fingernail. 'No. Although there is something about the symbol...something almost familiar...' He sighed. 'But it escapes me, still.'

'We found the same symbol on the Alp who was preying on my Granny,' I said. 'And that had been going on for decades. So whoever they are, they've been around a long time.'

Mrs Winchester tutted and shook her head. 'Preying on the elderly. Shameful!'

Klous looked thoughtful, his amphibian-like face pensive. 'Hmmm...'

'You have a theory?' Mr Gout asked.

'Not exactly.' The Klabautermann's round eyes bulged. 'But it's worrying, what with the real reason I came 'ere.'

'Real reason?' I narrowed my eyes. 'You said your ship–'

'I sank it, yeah. But that don't mean I wasn't heading here anyway. Things just got...

complicated.'

'Why?' I demanded. 'Why were you on your way here?' I felt a little lied to. I had been worrying I had led the strange creature right to Mr Gout's door – well, Mrs Winchester's door – and the whole time he had been on his way here anyway.

'Because I have a message for you,' Klous said, turning to Mr Gout, who paused his eating in surprise.

'Me?' he said around a hunk of bread. 'From whom?'

'From us. From the Kobold. We's a solitary species, most of the time, but we do get together, sometimes. At important moments, like. We had one such meeting a few weeks ago.'

'Fascinating. Do you have some sort of leadership? A council or elders, perhaps?'

'Somethin' like that. But we mostly just agrees on stuff anyway. We're usually of one mind.'

'And on this occasion that mind led you to me?'

'Right,' said Klous.

Mr Gout put aside his bowl and considered the little creature sitting next to him on the bench. 'In the old books,' he said, 'There is often mention of Kobold giving humans warnings. Warnings of dire danger.'

Klous shuffled uncomfortably. 'Never said it was a good message.'

'Well, good or dire, you had better let me have it,' Mr Gout said. 'I promise to give it my full consideration. After all you've been through to get here, it seems the least I can do.'

'Right…right.' Klous looked miserable. He seemed to avoid making eye contact with my master. 'Only the thing is…well, these prophecies are all very well and good when you don't know the people involved. But once you've met 'em…'

Mr Gout smiled kindly. 'Whatever it is, my friend, I promise not to take it personally. How about that?'

'You're going to die!' the Klabautermann wailed, wringing his clawed hands together, his spherical eyes watering.

'What!' Mrs Winchester and I cried in unison.

Mr Gout blinked at the creature. 'We all die, Klous,' he said calmly, his face neutral. 'Does your prophecy have any more details than that?'

Klous blew his nose into the sleeve of his coat. 'Something's coming, Mr Gout, sir. Something bad. You'll be the one to face it. And you'll lose. Tha's all we know.'

'How? How do you know that?' I demanded.

The Klabautermann shrugged. 'How does a bird fly?'

'Hollow bones and powerful wing muscles,' I snapped.

Klous glared at me. 'What I mean is, we're jus' born this way. We get brief glimpses. Snapshots of the future. It's like…' he paused, considering. 'It's sort o' like a shared dream. When it comes to us, it comes to us all.'

'When?' said Mrs Winchester. 'When is he supposed to die?'

Klous gave another shrug. 'Dunno. It's a prophecy, not a weather report.'

'Do you think it was supposed to be in the explosion? The booby trap?' I asked. 'Someone set that to go off if the curse was destroyed, and it seems to me that they sent the curse for you, Mr Gout.'

Mr Gout said nothing, just scratched his chin thoughtfully.

'Sent for him? What makes you say that?' Mrs Winchester asked.

'Think about it. Whoever sent that Zombie knew that there was a Klabautermann on the ship they chose because they shielded the Zombie from your magic, Klous. But why do that and not just choose another ship? It only makes sense if they chose the ship *because* Klous was onboard. And as the curse doesn't work on you, Klous, it means they wanted the curse to affect whoever was present at your destination.'

'Meaning they knew I was coming to see Mr Gout,' Klous said.

I nodded.

Mrs Winchester looked unconvinced. 'But if they knew all that, why didn't they shield the curse from Theo's detection, too? They must have known he'd be able to put a stop to it.'

'Because they wanted him to put a stop to it. They wanted you to be present when the curse was destroyed and the booby trap went off,' I said, looking at my master. 'We only survived because of Custard.'

Mr Gout didn't meet my eye. His face had that faraway look again.

'It all seems a bit convoluted,' Mrs Winchester said. 'There are easier ways to kill a person.'

'The prophecy wasn't about the curse,' Klous said.

'How do you know?' I asked.

The Kobold hung his head. 'Because Mr Gout is still alive. And our prophecies are never wrong.'

We sat in silence for some time after that, each digesting the news in our own way. Then, with no warning at all, Mr Gout heaved himself to his feet. 'Well, I think this calls for another bowl of cawl.'

I gaped at him. I did not know what to say. How could he be so cheery after receiving a death sentence?

Mrs Winchester knew exactly what to say. 'Theophilius Gout, you gluttonous pig! How can you still be thinking about your stomach at a time like this?'

Mr Gout fished a pocket watch out of his tweed jacket and looked at it quizzically. 'It's teatime,' he said, then his face split into a childlike grin. 'Ooh, I wonder if old Mal has any jam pudding on the go? I could just go for some of that! Anyone else?'

Mrs Winchester gave a tut of disgust and turned away. I shook my head mutely.

'Do...do you think he's got any pease pudding?' Klous asked, almost shyly.

Mr Gout slapped him heartily on the back, an action that almost knocked the little creature right off the bench. 'Only one way to find out, old boy!' he said. 'Come on.'

Once they had gone, an awkward silence fell over the bench. I sat at one end, Mrs Winchester at the other. I couldn't think of what to say to the woman. The sound of the waves and the gulls suddenly seemed very loud. But just as I decided that, perhaps, on further reflection, I was hungry after all, the woman spoke.

'Well,' she said, not looking at me but continuing to stare out to sea. 'Here we are then.'

'Yes,' I said.

'I have decided that, on balance, perhaps it is not a totally awful thing, you being here, girl,' she said, as if I hadn't spoken. 'You were brave. Back on the beach.'

'Um…right.' Was this an olive branch?

'I might even be tempted to admit,' she continued, still watching the waves. 'That having you around might be good for…good for the business.'

'Well, thank you. I will certainly try to make myself useful. And thank you for having me in your home…and for saving my life,' I said. The old woman nodded, just once, then lapsed back into silence. I fiddled with my thumbs for a moment, fighting with myself, then said, 'Mrs Winchester, is it really true that Mr Gout was cursed into forgetting where his own home is?'

This made the housekeeper turn to face me at last. She regarded me for a time, her expression unreadable. 'That's what he told you, is it?'

I nodded. 'And that he can't sleep under a proper roof.'

'Yes, it's true,' she said. 'Although it's not the half of it.'

'You mean there's more to the curse?'

'Theo is…a complicated man. I have known him now for a great many years. More than I'd care to admit. But even I know perhaps a third of what I suspect there is to know about him. You'll have noticed it by now, I reckon. How he is different from other folk.'

'When I first met him,' I said slowly. 'I felt… almost compelled to trust him. I told him things. Things I certainly wouldn't normally have shared with a complete stranger.'

Mrs Winchester chuckled softly. 'Most people do.'

'Is it…' I hesitated, not wanting to cause offence. But she finished my question for me.

'Magic?'

I nodded again.

'Truthfully, I'm not sure,' she said. 'He's a charismatic man. People like him. But sometimes… sometimes he'll get a look. As though he can see right through your skull to your innermost thoughts. He's dangerous. You should know that.' She held my gaze.

I smiled nervously. 'Dangerous? Surely–'

'Dangerous to know,' she cut me off. 'There are dark things out there in the world he walks. You've seen that already. You just be sure you're ready for… whatever might be coming.'

'It's funny. He said something similar to me himself, before I came here.'

'Well, he wasn't jesting. This ain't no life for normal, decent folk.'

I thought about everything that had happened to me since I first met Mr Gout. 'I think,' I said, 'That normal might be overrated.'

Mrs Winchester gathered up her skirts and got to her feet. 'Oh, certainly it is,' she said. 'Right up to the point you realise you can never go back to it. Come on, I'll buy you a cup of tea.'

And with that, she disappeared into the pub, leaving me alone on the bench. A gust of wind blew in off the rolling waves. I shivered.

THE END

Trussel and Gout will return in:
The White Owl of Thicklewood Hall

ACKNOWLEDGEMENT

This book took me a long time to write. I dashed out it's predecessor with out much thought to it's reception. When early readers were so glowing in their praise for it, I found myself frozen with the expectation that I might be able to do it again. I don't think I could have got over that self doubt with out the continued support of a few special people.

My wife Hayley was, as always, a rock. For your endless support and encouragement, I thank you.

My special thanks once again to Nicola, Hanna, and Helen, who offered both encouragement and pointers on the early drafts.

A huge thanks to Nick Hodgeson of Root-and-Branch editing, whose expert advise again polished this manuscript until it shone. Any remaining mistakes are, again, mine alone.

The #Writingcommunity on instagram have been an unending source of wisdom and support. The #booktok community on Tiktok have also been amazing in their enthusiasm for the release of this book. I thank you once more.

My heart felt thanks to my beta readers. I could not have done this without you all.

ABOUT THE AUTHOR

M.A.Knights

Hello. I'm M.A.Knights, an English writer living in the glorious countryside of wild west Wales. Here, the rugged cliffs, rolling hills and ever-changing sea inspire the worlds of my creation. After achieving a BSc in Countryside Conservation and an MSc in Geographic Information and Climate Change, I realised I am, in fact, not a scientist at all. It's the what-do-you-call-it? ... memory! Not what it used to be, don't you know? And what with all those numbers and things ... dreadful! Simply dreadful. So I've left the data crunching to those cleverer than I and instead have returned to the fantastical imaginings of my youth. I hope one day to lose myself in a world of my own creation.

Inspired by writers like Terry Pratchett, P.G.Wodehouse, Tom Holt and Jasper Fforde I revel in the creation of fantastical worlds full of improbable beasts and eccentric, larger than life characters.

Printed in Great Britain
by Amazon

36071197R00067